THE FIXER

THE FIXER SERIES #1

JACK WALKER

ONE

ICE RATTLED off the side of the glass from the shaking of his hand. No matter how hard he tried, he just could not stop the shaking. It was as if his hands were no longer his own. They had been taken over by his past and the dark memories that laid within him.

Taking a long pull from the glass of whiskey, he hoped to control his fears, but still the shaking wouldn't stop and he knew he couldn't drink himself blind, not while he still had a job to do. Calming his hand for just a moment he pulled a pack of cigarettes from his front pocket and patted the side of the box; a habit from years of smoking, though he never really knew why he did it. Struggling to get the cigarette into his mouth he took a deep breath and attempted to regain composure again. Lifting his hand, the cigarette fell from his trembling fingers and hit the floor as if discarded.

"Damn it!" he growled to himself.

Trying to fight was no use. It was going to happen, like it always did, but now was the worst possible time. In his own apartment and in the darkness of night he could fight it to the best of his abilities but now was a different story. Now people were relying on him and paid him good money to complete a job. Falling apart wasn't an option.

"Come on man! Hold it together."

Digging his fingers into the arms of the chair, sweat began to drip from his face and run down the back of his neck. The anticipation spiked his anxiety. Thrashing his head from side to side he tried to keep the flashbacks away, but for Michael Falau this had all become a torturingly regular way of life. He could feel the horror coming on and had yet to find a way to combat it. It did what it pleased, wreaking havoc over his mind and body, controlling every aspect of who he was and how he functioned. The desperate lone look in the man's eyes searched for answers that he had yet to find for more than eight long years.

The large man was built like a doorway, stronger than most and more cunning as well. With dark hair and dark eyes, he bore a scruffy exterior. An unshaven face and second-hand clothes were what most people saw first, just before they'd cross the street to avoid him. But now he sat in a wooden chair fighting the demons in his mind and praying they would leave him alone just this once.

Falau's eyes rolled back into his head as bits and pieces of the flashbacks started shooting through his mind like lightning bolts on a hot summer's night. Just as a lightning bolt cracked a random pattern through the night sky, so did the plagues of his mind, shifting to different directions and pulling in different memories from across the past, convoluting a way to make sense of it all and put it into perspective. How could one moment, just a fraction of a second, change a man's life? Disrupt an entire lifetime of achievement and hard work. Having it dashed away in a flash and create a crumbling mess of which once was a pillar of potential.

The image of a beautiful woman looking at him entered his head. He could see her sitting, facing him in the passenger seat of the car. She smiled with a deep love in her eyes, whispering words he could not hear. He desired to lean closer to her and hear her voice and feel her breath on his neck. Laughing along with her he turned to face her, no woman had ever looked more beautiful in his eyes. As she shifted herself to lean back against the car door, he pulled to a stop at a red light and leaned in to kiss her. Instead she grabbed him around the neck and hugged him, whispering, "I love you," into his ear. As she leaned back again the light turned green and he hit the gas, rolling into the intersection. Glancing back to her with a smile he watched as she tilted her head slightly to the side and gave a coy, playful smile in return.

Without any warning, he saw a pickup truck speeding toward them over her shoulder through the window behind her. Falau's expression changed to horror, as confusion spread over the woman's face. Her eyebrows furrowed at the center above her nose, causing a crinkle in her skin.

The pickup truck made no attempt to stop, crashing into them and impacting the passenger side door. The tortured screeching of twisting metal and shattering glass filled his ears, just as it had done on the day of the accident. There was no hesitation, there was no delay like in so many other dreams. It was in real time, as if he was still there sitting behind the wheel of the pickup truck, seeing the impact and feeling it through his body.

Falau jerked in his chair from the impact of his flashback as if he were living through it all over again. Letting out a pained moan he could feel the painful dream letting him go. It had done its job of abusing him. His eyes started to refocus as the last images of blood and pitiful screams filled his head. Gasping hard for air like a man who had just surfaced from too long underwater, his heart raced and he felt like he was going to vomit.

Drained from the battle in his mind Falau blinked his eyes rapidly trying to wash the images away, his clothes had now become soaked with sweat, and his eyesight stayed out of focus. Taking in a deep and long breath, looking down to his left hand, he tried to focus, seeing each finger individually rather than the mass of blob they had become in his blurred eyes.

Looking down at his right hand he was still clutching the whiskey glass and shaking like an out of rhythm drummer. He lifted the glass hard to his lips, forcing the drink as his hands shook. Tilting his head back, the glass crashed against his teeth. He forced the glass to his mouth and drank the remainder of the whiskey in one hit and dropped the glass onto the table next to him as if he had just defeated it in battle.

Clearing his head back into working order he reached over to the table and took a towel to wipe the sweat from his face. He wanted to scream into the towel and expel some of the frustration he felt, but now was no time for self-pity. Taking two deep breaths, he regained control of his breathing and finally felt like himself again. Composure was a hallmark for the man, always being able to control himself under the most difficult of situations. Straightening his shirt, he reached down wiping his hands on the side of the arms of the chair, trying to let some of the sweat that had accumulated roll off. Now is the time to be a professional, and now is the time, not to get caught up in his own past, but to do what he needed to do, to make money.

He stood from his chair and walked to a wooden door to his right. Leaning into the door he held his ear close, listening for any sound.

He heard a muffled moan. Falau looked down at his watch.

Right on time, he thought.

Picking up a backpack that rested next to the chair, the groans from the next room got louder and the sound of a man's mumbling voice cut through the air.

Picking up his glass again, he refilled it and downed the whiskey.

"Now is the time. All he needs is a little proper motivation. I can get the money and get the hell outta here." Falau downed another whiskey in a single large hit.

"I can do this," Falau whispered to himself.

TWO

TURNING and closing the door behind him, Falau entered a room that looked like an average basement in every home. The floor was made of cement and together with the stone walls formed the foundation of the structure. There was only one door to the room and the half windows were boarded up. The space was wide open and free from anything other than a table and a foldout chair. The clutter that normally would have been in any basement was gone. It was stripped down for a reason.

Walking over to the table he laid his backpack on it and opened the flap, but removed nothing. Pushing his hair back from his eyes he turned and sat down, laying his eyes on the man he captured just hours before. The corners of his lips rose and formed a sort of jagged smile that was out of place even for a man like Falau.

The man on the floor looked at Falau, trying to get his eyes to focus properly. He was young, only in his twenties. His hair was dark and his eyes a deep brown. He was handsome by any person's standards, but not so much that it set him apart from the crowd. He wore jeans and a t-shirt but was missing shoes and a belt. He looked like any other twenty-something trying to shake off a hard night of drinking but now held something different in his mind. The haze was thick and uncompromising not letting the young man regain his faculties the way he would normally after a night of partying.

Falau pulled out his pack of cigarettes and banged them against his hand, popping one from the opening. Hands now steady, he drew one from the pack using only his lips. As the cigarette left the pack it quivered in the tightness of his mouth like a man in a gangster movie. Striking a match, he cupped it in front of the cigarette and lit it.

"Oh, excuse me," Falau said, pulling the cigarette from his mouth, and holding it in front of him. "You mind if I smoke?"

A look of confusion and anger passed over the face of the man sitting on the floor. He leaned back and looked down at his hands, handcuffed to a thick chain, bolted deep into the cement floor. The chain was no more than two-feet long and had links that could not be destroyed by the biggest of bolt cutters. The links were four inches long and thicker than a cigar. The weight of the chain pulled at the young man even when he was not attempting to fight it.

The man pulled up the chain, frantically trying to yank it from the ground. Grunts and groans flew from his mouth as he put every shred of energy he had into trying to remove the bolt from its deep cement hole.

Rising to his knees, he grabbed the chain low and leaned back with all his strength. Once, twice, three times, but still nothing. The chain dropped from his now bleeding hands as his chest heaved up and down from his rapid breathing.

Sweat dripped from his nose and chin to the floor as he looked down at the ground seeing no difference despite his best efforts.

Falau sat motionless in the chair with his legs crossed and the cigarette still perched between his fingertips as he held it out in front of him.

"All you had to do was say no." Falau smiled, putting out the cigarette on the table.

Breaking his gaze from the cold hard cement of the floor, the man lifted his head and locked eyes with Falau.

"Why?" the man asked, holding his bound hands out in front of him. Confusion filled the man's eyes as he stared at his captor. An endless array of thoughts raced through the man's mind. Did he know this man from somewhere? Had he done him wrong? Could it be a twisted joke from his friends who waited on the other side of the door ready to laugh. Or was the man that sat in front of him insane and had captured him for pleasure.

"You made this happen. Not me," replied Falau in a matter-of-fact tone.

The man shook his head and looked side to side. He pulled again at the chain but with less force than before. His body was drained from the first round of pulling and it wasn't recovering the way that it normally would. Whatever the man used to drug him with had lasting effects that went beyond rendering him unconscious.

"I made this happen? Me? How could I make this happen?" stammered the young man trying to find some answers from the cryptic message he had just heard.

Falau reached for his backpack and turned it to him. Sliding one hand inside he removed a half-filled bottle of water. Cracking the seal, the rugged man removed the top and took a drink not looking at the man chained to the floor.

"You made it happen because of who you are. The kind of person you are. You have only yourself to blame," said Falau, speaking as if the young man already knew the answers that he was asking.

"You're insane. You have the wrong man. I'm just a normal guy," explained the man, turning to Falau, his voice changing from anger, to pleading, and finally begging to be understood. "Are you going to kill me?"

Falau felt a pulse pound hard through his temples. It was the flashbacks again. He strained his eyes to maintain his focus and not regress back into the horror. A female voice echoed inside his mind. *You did this. You killed me.*

Falau quickly stood up, shaking his head. "It's up to you if you live or die."

"What? You mean I can just say I want to go and I can go?" questioned the young man, simplifying the situation in the same manner a child would.

"I didn't say that. I said it was up to you if you die. You need to be smart and work with me," said Falau nodding to the young man with a reassuring smile.

"What do you need to know? I will tell you anything. Just let me go," begged the young man.

"What's your name?" asked Falau, now sounding more like a detective interrogating a prisoner.

"William Jefferson. But everyone calls me Billy," said the young man with confusion in his voice. "You don't know my name?"

"Where did you go to college?" asked Falau disregarding the question from Billy.

"Tridon. In the city," said the young man sheepishly.

Falau started to pace back and forth in front of the man, occasionally glancing at him out of the corner of his eye. Bringing his hand up, he scratched at the scruff that covered his chin after a week without shaving.

"Tridon. They are known for a lot of wild parties. Bet that you have some great stories after four years there," said Falau letting his voice sound more jovial and continuing to move the emotional tone of the conversation, keeping Billy off balance.

"Well, yeah. We all had a lot of fun. Why do you want to know about that? It was a long time ago," said Billy.

"Tridon is an expensive school. You must come from some money," said Falau again making his tone harsh and aggressive. "A scrub like you couldn't afford to go there from working summers, and you don't look like you could win any kind of scholarship. You're too dumb and too fat for anything like that."

"Yeah... My parents do okay... Money I can get you. Just let me go, and I'll get as much as you want," said Billy brightening his tone.

Halting his pacing, Falau turned to Billy and crouched down into a low squat. "One of those parties got a little too fun, didn't it? You had a few too many drinks one night and hopped in the nice little BMW Mommy and Daddy got you and you drove home."

"No! I would never drink and drive!" said Billy pulling his eyes away from the man.

"You killed a girl less than a quarter-mile from your parents' house. A girl who lived in your neighborhood all her life," said Falau in a calm and relaxed manner that did not fit the accusation that he had placed on Billy.

"No! Noooo!" screamed Billy as he started to yank hard

on the chain trying to free himself from the fate that awaited him. "That wasn't me. I was asleep when that happened..."

Rising up from his crouch, Falau methodically walked to the table and reached into the backpack again. His hands roamed the inside of the backpack looking for just the right object to continue his investigation.

"Please don't kill me! I didn't do a thing. I swear it!" yelled Billy as his mind put together what was happening, but his words had not created so much as a glance from that man who had taken him captive.

Turning around and walking back to Billy, Falau held a plain tan folder in his hand. The folder was slim and appeared to hold a small number of papers.

"Billy, you're making this very hard on yourself. Look at this picture."

Falau held up a picture of an attractive young female, perhaps in her late teens. Her brown hair fell onto her shoulders and she smiled the smile of someone without a care in the world. She wore a cheerleader uniform and had one arm raised into the air. The all-American girl next door. A gentle beauty that did not need makeup or expensive clothing to draw attention from the boys of her school.

"This is Erica Snell. But you know that, don't you Billy? She was killed the night you hit her with your car," said Falau pointing to the girl in the picture.

"No! No! It wasn't me," Billy cried, shaking his head and starting to wail. "You need to believe me. I didn't do a thing!"

"Billy, look at this other picture. That's your car... look at the damage to the front passenger side. You hit something while going very fast. What was it you told the police you had hit?" asked Falau as if he didn't already know the answer.

"A dog. And it's true. I did hit a dog! They run all over the place in my neighborhood! Nobody keeps them chained up!" said Billy trying to lift his hand to point outside but was stopped by the strength of the chain.

"That must've been one hell of a big dog. I have hit deer by accident, and my car didn't have that much damage. From what I understand the police never came to question you that night. The car was seen by the insurance company the next day, and was in and out of the shop in two days. When I hit the deer I was stuck in a rental for over a week," said Falau changing his voice to confusion at how such a situation could exist.

"My dad knows the guy who owns the auto body place and told him that I needed the car for school. Please believe me... I would never kill that girl. I even used to babysit her," said Billy dropping his head and looking at the floor.

Climbing to his feet, Falau walked over to the table and tossed the file on it. Pausing to get his thoughts, he felt no oncoming rush from the flashbacks. Taking a sip from the water bottle he turned back around to question Billy again.

"Seems that your father knows a lot of people in town. He's a real estate developer, right?" asked Falau.

"Yeah," replied Billy. "What does my dad have to do with anything?"

"Lots of money in that field. You can also make other people a lot of money if you tell them the right projects to get in on," said Falau letting out a small laugh. "It can be really beneficial when one hand washes the other."

"I guess so," said Billy not raising his eyes from the floor.

"Permits, and getting things by inspectors, means a guy needs to know a lot of people at City Hall. Contacts like that would be very useful when his son kills a girl with his car," said Falau.

"I said I didn't kill her!" screamed Billy, his voice again switching from fear to anger, and again, he yanked on the chain that did not give him one inch.

Falau was sure if he had broken free he would have attacked him rather than run for the door. He was losing his composure and being broken down bit by bit. Falau smiled.

"It's a fact that he owns the building the repair shop is in. 'Daddy' built the development that most of the cops, including the chief, live in. Did he give them all a break on housing costs due to their public service?" asked Falau in more of a statement than a question.

"My dad is a very well-respected man. He does wonderful things for people!" said Billy defending his father.

"Like letting you get away with murder! You killed Erica with your car! Just admit it!" snapped Falau pointing his index finger at the young man.

"No! I never did that! I hit a dog!" said Billy looking down at the ground, his voice becoming softer and softer. "Some other person hit Erica, not me. I was asleep."

An exasperated sigh left Falau's mouth and he stood up. Shaking his head, he walked over to the backpack and pulled out a folded towel. Placing it gently on the table Falau stretched his neck looking up to the ceiling and rolling it from side to side.

"What do you have there? What are you going to do?" asked Billy, flinching at the sound of metal hitting metal.

Without turning or lifting his head, Falau unrolled the towel to reveal several tools. The tools had a history with the man and had proven effective every time they had been called upon.

"Proper motivation," said Falau clearly and calmly.

Spreading the tools out on the towel, Falau took inventory of what he had. Pliers, hammer, clamps, nails, and a straight edged razor.

"What the hell is that supposed to mean?" barked Billy.

"It means I'm going to help you find the truth," replied Falau, turning around with the straight edged razor in his hand, opened and in the locked position. The blade was 4-inches long and shone, despite the limited light of the basement. The young man's eyes locked on the steal that was moving toward him causing him to pull back before the chain stopped his escape.

Terror fell over Billy's face. "No! Come on, man! Whatever you want, I can get it for you! Just don't do this!"

Falau walked over, slowly closing the gap between Billy and himself, the razor held firm in his right hand and his eyes locked on Billy's. This was always the hardest moment. It was the time where he could just walk away, move on with his life, and keep the blood off his hands both figuratively and literally.

"Did you or did you not kill Erica Snell, with your car, when you were drunk driving?" asked Falau gripping the razor tight in his hand.

"No! I didn't do it. What, do you have cops watching me, trying to bust me for that? I didn't do it! What the hell was she doing out that late anyways?" asked Billy trying to convince the man he was not guilty of the crime.

As Falau moved closer, Billy got to his feet, but the chain kept him from standing up straight. His hands were still down by his thighs and he was unable to raise them any further. He yanked the chain in desperation, trying again to rip it from the ground. The cuffs that held his wrists pulled into his skin cutting it and drawing a steady stream of blood that the young man did not feel in his moment of desperation.

Immediately Falau kicked as hard as he could, directly into Billy's stomach. The young man dropped to his knees and gasped for air. Falau set himself again, and kicked Billy hard, this time in the face, spraying blood from his nose and knocking him to the floor. The short length of the chain stopped his falling back and instead snapped him to the ground in a heap as his body could go no further.

Moving with explosive speed Falau stepped on the chain close to Billy's feet as the young man tried to get up, and used his knee to drive him onto his back on the ground.

Falau held the razor within an inch of Billy's eyes. Twisting the blade side-to-side, Billy's eyes locked on the unyielding steel that could do so much damage.

"Do you remember killing Erica Snell now?" asked Falau speaking no louder than a whisper.

"Yes!" screamed Billy "It was late! Why would she be out there at that time of night! She should've been wearing something bright! I couldn't see her! It wasn't my fault!"

Falau stared down at Billy, now starting to cry. Billy's body had now gone limp giving up the fight with the chain that held him. Leaning back, Falau rose to his feet and pulled Billy to his knees.

"So, you admit you killed her?" asked Falau in a matter of fact tone.

"Yes. I killed her. I'm sorry. It was an accident," said Billy softly making it clear he had been broken.

Slowly turning away, Falau suddenly reached back and

grabbed a handful of Billy's hair, pulling himself in close. He ran the razor down Billy's right cheek, leaving a laceration 6-inches long and very deep. For a moment, it looked like a valley between two mountain ranges, but soon the valley filled with blood. Billy screamed out in pain as Falau pushed him to the floor and wiped the blade on the pants of the injured man.

"Oh God! Why? Why did you do that? I told you everything!" cried Billy, reaching up and trying to stop the bleeding. "I'm going to need stiches! This will be a permanent scare!"

"It's a reminder of what you did. Every time you look in the mirror you will remember," said Falau with cold detachment as he packed up his tools at the table.

The only door in the room opened, revealing a man and a woman in their fifties slowly entering and unable to take their eyes off Billy.

"Mr. and Mrs. Snell?" questioned Billy with amazement. "It was an accident! I swear it was an accident! I had too much to drink! Everyone drinks and drives! Why was she out there? You should have kept her inside!"

The couple stared back at Billy, not saying a word. A mixture of hate, anger, and pity etched their faces. The young man who had stood in their back yard with his family enjoying a barbecue now was trying to explain how their daughter was at fault for him killing her with his car.

Mr. Snell put out his hand to stop his wife, as he continued making his way to Billy, who lay crying on the floor in a pool of his own blood.

"You killed her. I heard you admit it. After all these years it took this to make you do the right thing. Now you're going to have to pay," said Mr. Snell as hatred was the only thing that was holding his tears back.

"I said I was sorry. What about forgiveness for me? You're Christian. You have to forgive me, it's in the Bible!" yelled Billy, grasping to anything that might let him taste freedom once more.

"The Bible also says an eye for an eye," said Mrs. Snell in a slow, monotone voice.

Throwing his backpack over his shoulder Falau took two steps towards the door when Mrs. Snell's voice stopped him in his tracks with a request.

"$10,000 to kill him now."

"That's not our agreement," said Falau, turning to look at Mr. Snell.

"I want another agreement. I have an unmarked .38 revolver right here. Pull the trigger and $10,000 in cash is yours," said Mr Snell extending his hand holding the gun in his palm.

"That's not what I do," responded Falau, turning away from the Snells. "That's not who I am."

"Of course that's who you are. Anyone can see it in you. You didn't need to cut him, but you did and you liked doing it. You can't change who you are," said Mr Snell cutting to the soul of Falau.

With Mr. Snell's words still hanging in the air, another sharp pain jabbed into Falau's temple. The flashback was soft and distant, but unmistakable, as the voice of a woman saying, "You killed me... it was your fault," rang in his ears once again.

"No!" snapped Falau, taking another step toward the door.

Reaching out and grabbing Falau by the arm, Mr. Snell

shouted, "$20,000!" causing Falau to stop again and turn back.

"If you want him dead so bad, you pull the trigger," said Falau, ripping his arm from Mr. Snell's grip. "I'm not a killer!"

Falau walked across the room and through the door, stopping only to grab the bottle of whiskey he'd been drinking earlier, shoving it into his backpack. Making his way up the back steps to the door his head started to throb. He knew that the flashbacks would be coming again, and soon. Turning the handle to the outside door, he heard a single gunshot from the basement follow by a muffled scream. Falau stepped out into the light, happy to leave that place behind.

THREE

FALAU MADE his way down the sidewalk of Massachusetts Avenue in Boston. The sky was filled with clouds that threatened the day with rain at any moment and hid the sun from the people of the city.

Carrying a bag of groceries, he looked at the sky hoping he would just about make it back in time. Making his way up the streets he looked at the old, rundown brownstones and wondered how wonderful the neighborhood was when all the brownstones were occupied by individual families. At one time it housed the Boston elite, but that was a long time ago. Now the buildings were broken up into six to nine apartments, a common bathroom on each floor. Not quite a boardinghouse, just one step above. The buildings were covered in the stains of years of car exhaust and pollution, and the intricate wooden doors were scarred with graffiti. The neighborhood was now the location of Boston's working and non-working poor.

"Mr. Falau is back again!" said an elderly African American man sitting on the steps of Falau's building. The man's hair had started to turn gray on the sides and his face was drawn from years of hard times. His clothing was worn down and lacked any style, but despite it all, he still saved a smile for Falau when he saw him. "Lucky you didn't get caught in the rain."

"Grady! How goes it, old friend?" said Falau, reaching out to shake hands.

Grady was quick to also reach out, and use two hands, to shake hands with his friend. "I've something you will like," he said with a sly smile.

"Oh, you do?" said Falau. "Well I don't see Miss Massachusetts sitting next to you so what is it?"

"Yes Sir, you will like this," replied Grady, reaching to his side and pulling up a bottle covered in a paper bag. The spout of the bottle poked out of the top of the bag, missing its cap. Grady had obviously been sampling the surprise before Falau got home. "Whiskey. Your favorite. And it ain't none of that cheap stuff. This is top shelf. Well maybe not top shelf, but second from top. I was thinking maybe you could join me out here and we can make our way through this bottle. You know what they say... if you drink alone you're a drunk, but if you drink with someone else you're a friend."

"That sounds great. Thanks for thinking of me," replied Falau. "Give me thirty minutes and I'll be back down with a few beers as chasers."

Passing Grady, Falau patted him on the back and took out his keys.

"Oh, Falau, there was a white guy here earlier looking for you. Said you were an old friend but he be dressed like a bill collector. So, I didn't trust him and said you were gone," said Grady with a sound of distrust in his voiced.

"Did he say who he was?" asked Falau.

"Don't know. I asked him, he said he would just catch up with you later. He turned a lot of heads pulling up in that fancy car. You're the only white guy around here so the whole neighborhood is wondering who you done wrong to have a heavy like that sent after you," said Grady letting his voice turn to concern. "If you need to lay low the YMCA is right around the corner. Good place to sleep and not be found."

"Grady, you know I keep to myself. Probably some jackass serving me with papers for defaulting on a credit card. They can sue me if they want, I have no money to give them. You can't bleed a stone," replied Falau with a snicker.

"You got that right. You live down here just to keep it real," Grady said laughing at his own joke.

"Yeah. My other house is in Wellesley!" said Falau. "I am really one of the rich guys."

The two men laughed as Falau opened the door and pushed his way inside, starting up three flights of steps with the bag of groceries pulled in close to his body. The hallway smelled of urine, a smell all too familiar. Falau had learned early on that the mothers would tell their children to urinate in the hallway because it would stop the drug dealers from setting up shop in their building and selling drugs.

Unlocking his door he walked into his studio apartment. He sighed at just how bleak his life had become as he walked across the room and put the bag of groceries on a small table. Across the room sat an old sofa, it had some patches covered with duct tape and a sheet pulled over it to hide the holes. A lamp sat on the floor without a shade. Next to the window on the far side of the floor laid a mattress without a box spring. No sheet covered the mattress. Scattered on the floor next to the bed was an ashtray, several discarded cigarettes, alcohol bottles, and the want ads from the newspaper.

The big man started to unload the groceries when he heard the toilet flush in his bathroom. Freezing up, Falau attempted to assess the situation, carefully listening for footsteps or any noise that might divulge what was happening. Moving next to the table he crouched down, sure that the thief had heard him and had flushed the toilet as a way to let him know he was there. He probably expected whoever was in the main room to flee the apartment as soon as he heard the noise. But Falau had no intention of leaving.

"Mr. Falau. I'm going to come out now. I mean you no harm. I would just like to talk with you. It's been a long time since we've had a talk," said the voice that held some familiar sounds.

"Come out, but position your hands where I can see them. You do anything I don't like and I'll shoot you," said Falau bracing himself for a fight.

"Shoot me? You don't have a gun," replied the voice. "You don't recognize my voice?"

The voice rang familiar in Falau's ears, but it had changed. It brought with it a feeling of safety and comfort. The feeling of connection and belonging. All things that have been absent from his life for a long time.

"It's been over ten years. Bet my voice is deeper now. We were just kids back then," said the voice continuing to give him hints without revealing who he was.

With no effort at all, Falau's mind opened with a flood of information at the sound of his old best friend though the doorway.

"Tyler? Is that you?" asked Falau with amazement.

The handle on the bathroom door turned and the door

slowly opened, revealing a tall strong man in his late twenties. His hair was cut short and he wore a tailored suit. His hands were in the air as he'd been instructed to do, but he wore a smile on his face that did not show any fear at all.

"Don't shoot," joked Tyler lowering his hands. "I'm just here to seal all your prized possessions."

Walking across the room, Falau reached his hand out to his old friend, who reciprocated. The two men hugged and then looked one another over, appraising how their friend had aged over the years.

"Look at you, man. A suit. In shape. Looks like you've been doing well," exclaimed Falau feeling genuine pride in how his friend looked.

"I am. But I have a good place to work and they help take care of me," said Tyler letting his eyes drift up and down on Falau.

Walking to the sofa, Falau motioned for his friend to join him.

"I don't have that much time," said Tyler placing his hand out to show he would move no further.

"Okay. And how did you find me? Why come here after all this time?" questioned Falau cutting to the point as he always did with his longtime friend.

"Finding you was easy," said Tyler. "The Internet knows everything. I'm here to offer you a job."

"You remember everything from when you were young?" asked Falau unsure of how his past was intersecting the moment he was now having.

"Yeah. I set up a little system to help with that after I got out," replied Tyler. "Never heard another word about it."

Looking at the sofa, Tyler's eyes worked their way across the room, taking in all there was to see. "We go way back, so

I'm going to be blunt. Look around man. This sucks! This is no way for you to be living."

"It's not that bad. Jobs have been hard to find, and this is just temporary," said Falau trying to soften just how bad his apartment was.

"Five years temporary? That's not just a transition. You're stuck like this. A man with your experience and skills should not be in this situation," Tyler said, with all the sympathy of an angry teacher. "I have a way out of this for you."

"Who said I'm looking for a way out of anything. The people around here are good people, and maybe, just maybe, I like it here," snapped Falau feeling the defensiveness rise up in his body. His home may be bad but it was still his home. "You show up here after ten years and insult the way I live? The door is right there if this place isn't good enough for you."

Raising an eyebrow at the aggression, Tyler leaned toward his old friend. "I meant no offense. Just expecting you to be in a better spot. I know about the part-time job you did recently, and thought you were getting a good income from that."

"What part-time job?" asked Falau.

"Erica Snell," replied Tyler. "You remember the name don't you?"

"How did you know about that?" asked Falau feeling off balance now that Tyler had dropped Erica's name.

"We know everything. I know that Mr. Snell came to you after speaking with a cop who I'm friends with," said Tyler with a sly smile.

"You set that job up for me? Why?" asked Falau

realizing that the wheels for Tyler had been turning well before he set foot in Falau's home.

"Things just worked out. I found you, and figured you could use the money. I knew that you could handle the job," said Tyler without acknowledging that the job had led to a young man's torture and death.

Pulling himself from the sofa, Falau walked across the room, searching his mind for why Tyler would've acted in that manner. Looking to his old friend he asked, "What's the job?"

"Well, it's not exactly legal. But the work is good and it makes you feel good about what you're doing. That's what you're looking for, isn't it?" asked Tyler already sure of what the answer was.

"Yeah. What's the job?" asked Falau, more insistent.

"Okay. I'll tell you, but let me make one thing clear, what you're about to hear does not go beyond you and me. If I tell you this, you must keep it to yourself forever. If you say anything about it to anyone, at any time, there will be extreme consequences. Do you understand?" asked Tyler with a firmness to his voice Falau had only heard a few times before. "This is no game and the people I work for can't afford to have their secrecy broken. Make no mistake this is a life or death promise you're about to make. Sure you want to know?"

"Yes."

"Even if it could cost you your life?" asked Tyler.

"Yes."

"The job is simple to explain but hard to accomplish," said Tyler, standing up. Sliding his hands into his pockets he went on, "There are nine judges from around the world.

They make up a group that takes a second look at some cases."

"What do you mean, a second look?" asked Falau having his interest sparked "Are they part of an appeals court? Are you looking for a bounty hunter?"

Tyler raised his hand stopping Falau from saying more. It was natural to ask questions but he knew that it would be easier for the big man to listen to the information and process it on his own.

"Nobody knows who the judges are. They only speak to one person. They look at cases where they know justice has not been served for numerous reasons. They need to re-try these people, but they need to do that in a more secretive way," said Tyler trying to make the operation sound normal.

Falau moved over to the window and looked outside, still listening to what Tyler had to say. He could feel the tension starting to build up inside him as he anticipated what Tyler would say next.

"That's where you come in. They like these defendants to be brought in for retrial. As you would guess, they're not willing to do that, so they need to be helped to come back in. Basically, we take the scum that gets let off on technicalities, and give them a trial without all the crap," said Tyler. "The new trials are done without all the restraints of a normal court room. Justice is what's the focus of these trials."

"You mean you kill them," said Falau, turning back to look at Tyler.

"Not always. Some have even gone free. The judges just want the right outcome not the outcome that is written to the letter of the law. That's all they care about. This is the purest form of justice you could have. For you, it's a chance to be on the right side of good. You can help right the wrongs that the courts screw up so often. You're not a vigilante. You're an agent of change... for the better," said Tyler knowing the right words would move his friend toward seeing things his way.

Falau pushed back the hair from his eyes while still looking at the street down below. He couldn't believe that he was speaking with Tyler about this kind of a job. *You should be sitting on the step with Grady and drinking his one-shelf-below-the-top-shelf-whiskey and laughing,* he thought.

"Those days are gone for me. I can't handle that anymore. Too old and too slow," said Falau. "You should be talking to some young guy who still has the wherewithal for that kind of thing."

"You just did it the other day with Billy. I'm not saying it's the same as that snot nosed frat boy. Stakes are higher but it's the same basic idea. You can do it. We need a guy who can work alone and with others. A guy like you understands the art of cover. A guy like you knows the ins and outs of this work," said Tyler moving closer to his old friend. "It's what you know and what you're damn good at."

Turning back to the room, Falau smiled at his longtime friend. "I can't. It's just not for me."

"I can understand that. But I would regret it if I didn't tell you everything. The pay is $25,000 per job. Minimum. And you get to be one of the good guys," said Tyler. "I know you're not all about money but it could change your life."

"That's a lot of money. I don't make that much in a year," replied Falau, looking down at the floor. "But I just can't do it. I need to live a normal life. I can't get involved with that kind of mess again. Your secret is safe with me though. I will take it to the grave."

"Falau, you can't have a normal life. Not after what we

lived through. I'm sure you have a lot of the same problems I do, and the only thing that lets me sleep at night is this work. You need to think about that. I know the dreams haunt you the way they haunt me. The pain is more than I ever thought it would be but I'm offering you a chance to let go of some of the hate that is deep down inside you. Your experiences make you who you are but that's not the guy I once knew," explained Tyler. The sharp dressed young man walked across the room and pulled a business card from his pocket. "There's a number on here and I'm the only one who ever picks up the phone. If you change your mind I'm just a call away. I would love to work with you again, old friend. Take care."

"You too," said Falau taking the card and looking at the number on it. Worrying that the temptation to call would be too strong, Falau placed the card on the coffee table as he watched his friend walk out the door.

FOUR

UNBUCKLING HIS SUIT JACKET, as he stepped into the black Mercedes, Tyler let his eyes drift up and look at the window that held Falau. The man that he had known for so long had dropped such a long way. No longer was he the man that he'd known when he was younger, willing to take on any chance and any task in order to prove himself as the best. Now he was a drunken shell of the friend that he once knew and had become apathetic to his own life.

Closing the door behind him, Tyler slid the key into the ignition of the Mercedes starting it up and bringing the engine roaring to life. By anybody who had the slightest knowledge of cars knew that this engine had been worked on and was more than just stock. It had a ferociousness that pushed up inside it, showing its power to anyone who would question it.

Jumping the car from the curb, Tyler pressed the gas feeling the instantaneous grab of the wheels pushing him up Massachusetts Avenue. He hit the button to pull the inner cover of the sun roof away to let the sunshine beat down upon him without opening the roof completely.

"What the hell, Falau?" said Tyler to himself, shaking his head. "I knew it was bad, but I didn't think it was this bad. You've let it all just fall apart."

Taking the turn up onto route three, Tyler let himself head south bound in order to clear his head and have a chance to speak with his superiors.

"This should be a great conversation," said Tyler, turning on the radio system. He connected it to his phone that had a private link within it to talk to the leaders in the System.

The ring sounded several times before it connected.

"Yes?" said the voice on the far end of the phone that had been computer modulated to sound like nothing more than an automated machine.

"It's Tyler," said the young man, dropping the car into fifth gear and jumping into the left lane to pass the slow driver in front of him. "I wanted to give you all an update on what's happening with my friend."

"Are you in a secure setting?" asked the voice on the far end.

"This is about as secure as you can get it," said Tyler, having a slight smile at his ingenious way of routing phone calls.

The call from Tyler's phone jumped up to the heavens on its satellite link and then bounced to four other satellites before dropping back down in Lisbon, Portugal. From there, it jetted around the world linking through different countries and different phone systems, before finally finding its target after thirty relocations.

"I'm going about seventy miles an hour right now so I don't think anybody that was following me would be able to get away with it without me noticing, and as far as tracing the phone call, good luck to them locking onto me as I'm driving."

"Well, my read outs at this end tell me we're totally secure," said the voice that now seemed more willing to have an ongoing conversation.

"I think you'd wanna know some information on my buddy and his willingness to work with us," said Tyler, staring out the front window and focusing on the next car in front of him. Looking down to the speedometer, it read ninety miles an hour. If he wanted to maintain cover, there's no way he could drive with the aggressiveness that he loved so much.

"You know we're tracking you, right?" said the voice at the other end of the phone.

"I was sure of it," said Tyler. "Don't tell me, you think I'm driving too fast, and then I'm just drawing attention to myself."

A chuckle arrived on the other end of the phone before the voice began to speak again. "We've gone down this road a lot, haven't we, Tyler? I bet you're going to tell me that you're driving so fast to make sure that you're alone and to make sure that nobody is trying to track your call. Every time you say the same thing. Or could it be that you just love high performance vehicles and seeing what they can do?"

"Can't it be both?" Tyler asked hoping that the man on the other end of the phone would take the comment in jest.

"Well, nothing is like a new car," said the voice on the other side of the phone. "I think anybody can enjoy the aesthetic beauty and the engineering prowess that goes into building a car like that. Mercedes has a long history of making some outstanding automobiles," said the voice on the other end of the phone. "And with the special modifications you make to the cars you like to drive, it's a wonder that the thing can't take off into space."

"So you know about the modifications?" asks Tyler.

"Well, Tyler, you know we monitor everything. And if we just follow you, we can see that that car makes moves that the normal Mercedes doesn't," said the voice.

"For a minute there, I thought you had something tracking inside my car," said Tyler, trying to create some levity with the voice on the other side of the phone.

"What? Like the fact that you have three quarters of a tank of gas left in the car, and that you're traveling currently at seventy-five miles an hour, southbound, on Route 3, crossing Milton."

"You *are* tracking the car!"

"You might wanna look into getting your oil changed. It's been over 3000 miles," said the voice, letting out an audible laugh, which was a rarity on these phone calls.

"I should bring the car in to you guys for servicing since you watch it so closely."

"We watch everything closely," said the voice. "It means all of our lives."

The levity had left the voice of the member of the System on the other end of the phone. Even with its automated tone, it had become deadly serious and the words that were spoken were never so true. For a secret underground organization, there was more than enough trouble to get into with the authorities and other groups looking to make their mark on the world. If discovered, the System would be viewed simply as a murdering terrorist organization that had decided to take vigilante justice to a whole new level. The charges would be swift and devastating for all involved, that would more than likely end up with a life in prison or execution.

"Well, Falau has turned me down, but you know how that goes. Most of them turn me down the first time," said Tyler, drumming his fingers on the steering wheel. "He might come around, but the guy's in a very different place than I remember him being in."

"Well, you know I'm gonna make you explain that a little bit more," said the voice. "How much did you divulge to this man?"

"Just about everything," said Tyler. "I let him know about the organization and I let him know about what we do. I gave him no details on any missions or any actions that we've ever taken, but he gets the general idea."

"You know that I always trust your judgment Tyler, but if this guy is as rough around the edges as you say, do you think it was a good idea to let him know what we do and how we do it?" asked the voice.

"I can honestly say that no matter how messed up Falau is, he would never rat me out," said Tyler. "We've gone down far too many roads together for him to roll over on me on anything. He's saved my life and I've saved his more than a dozen times each, so I don't think this guy would ever let people know what I told him. And besides, who would believe him?"

"Give me a little more detail on this man. We just have some broad strokes, and he has very little information available."

"Well, you know the highlights. He's been working a mediocre job, just barely getting by," said Tyler, merging with the traffic coming up I95 and getting on the straightaway toward Cape Cod on Route 3. "He's really had a lot of struggles and the situation with the girl years ago seems to be haunting him still."

"Did you find out anything more about that?" asked the voice.

"Not really," said Tyler, knowing he missed an opportunity to press on Falau to see his response. "I'm not sure if he was engaged to the girl or if it's someone he had been dating, but with the little bit of surveillance footage I was able to dig up from the surrounding places around him during that time, it shows that she had been with him quite a bit. The problem is, this far after the fact, most of that footage is gone or has been taped over."

"So let's cut to brass tacks, Tyler, what's going on with the guy?" asked the voice. "We can't have any mistakes, and when I say any mistakes, I mean even the smallest. It'll be your ass hanging out if this guy comes aboard then screws the whole thing up. We'll have to cut ties in every way with everybody, and I think you know what that entails."

"The secrecy of the System stands above everything," said Tyler. "The day I joined this organization, I understood that, and I understand it today. And in no way would I allow anyone to divulge what we do and the impact we make on the world around us. You can count on me that I'm totally faithful to the System and there's no other loyalty I have that is stronger than that."

"That might be true, Tyler, but the problem is, this is an old friend, not just someone you're hiring," said the voice. "And old friendships have a way of controlling people. They have a way of making sure you remember the connection to them more than your connection to other things. That's what I worry about, this man has saved your life, and this man has been a part of your life, what happens if the decision has to be made between him and the System?"

"The answer is the System," said Tyler. "I pointed out Falau because I think he can do the best work for us for what we need to do. He's a skilled Black Ops man that has had numerous missions in hostile territories with hostile targets. He's the guy they would send in before everybody else. If you rely on me, then you can rely on him."

"That's all very reassuring but we started this conversation with you telling me that you had some question marks about your meeting with him," said the voice, unable to show emotion through the automation. "Tell me more about this guy, I'm not so sure I want him in our ranks."

"The biggest issue is the booze," said Tyler. "I've had him watched for a while now, and he has a daily drinking problem. The man drinks so much that he staggers up the streets and can barely open the door of his apartment. The drinking seems to be basically every day and it's dictating much of what he does in his life."

"Is he homeless and on the street?" asked the voice.

"No, he's constantly trying to either find a job or working at a job. The alcohol doesn't seem to have any effect on him getting up, going to a work and then doing his best on the job," said Tyler. "His biggest struggle is that he's attempting to do some manual labor and he's connected to nobody but himself. He's not in the union and he's made no attempt to get in. It appears to me that he's just trying to do whatever it takes to get by and to keep as low stressed as possible."

"So he's had no attempts to rise in the ranks in the jobs that he takes?" asked the voice.

"That's exactly right," said Tyler, nodding his head to nobody in the car. "The most recent job he had was doing labor work for a construction team. Numerous times they gave him the opportunities to take on more responsibility after seeing his abilities, but every time he rejected it. He shows no desire to improve himself or anything around him."

"And so when it comes firing time, he gets let go because he does just enough to get by," said the voice. "But that *just enough* doesn't save him when it comes time to crunch the numbers and see if the company is making a profit."

"That's exactly right. It's like he sets himself up for failure, he doesn't believe he deserves to be higher up in any of the jobs he works, he places himself at the bottom on purpose," said Tyler. "I'm not Sigmund Freud but this one's pretty easy to see. The guy is beating himself up for the past accident with the girl, and he's never been able to let it go."

"And you want us to take on this man?"

"I sure do. We're the ones that can bring him back to doing what he does best," said Tyler. "And I feel like that if we do that, he'll become a very loyal asset to us."

"This organization isn't about helping people's mental health, Tyler," said the voice, causing Tyler to squint his eyes, looking at the radio as if the man's voice and his face were inside it. "We can't just be helping this guy because he's your old buddy. And we can't send him out on a mission not knowing if he's going to screw it up. If this guy gets caught, and decides to talk and tell people who we are and what we do, it could be disastrous for everybody involved."

"Sir, if you leave this man with me, I can assure you that he will perform the duties that I ask him to in an exemplary way," said Tyler. "I've been to battle with this man, I've seen what he can do."

"But what about the covert stuff? That's what we're about, keeping it quiet, keeping it quick, and not leaving a trace. Can your friend do all of that or is this something that we're going to have to worry about with him, that he makes big splashes and shows himself to the world?" said the voice at the other end of the phone. "You know our standard. No attention. Not now, not ever."

Tyler smiled at the idea of Falau drawing attention to himself. The big man that he had spent so many hours with was never one to pull the attention toward himself, but rather he would consistently deflect praise that he well-deserved and put it on other people. Being in the spotlight was not his style or desire. He simply wanted to do what was good and help those that needed help.

"Sir, I can tell you that Falau is no fame jockey. He doesn't want anybody or anything to know what he's doing, even if he's just going to the grocery store," said Tyler, smiling at his own small joke. "I can guarantee you that this man will do everything that is asked of him, and well within the parameters of the mission assignment, or he'll die trying."

"You're risking a lot here, Tyler," said the voice. "You've spent a lot of years moving yourself up through the ranks, and being placed in the highest position possible without being a judge."

"I'm aware of that, Sir, and I don't feel like this move will tarnish that at all," said Tyler, trying to reassure the man at the far end of the phone.

"And you're willing to risk everything on this? You're even willing to risk the System, as an organization on your old friend from the past?"

"Yes, I am, Sir," said Tyler. "I believe in this guy, and I believe in what he can do, he's smart and skilled, he just needs something in his life that's gonna show him that he's not a loser and that he can come back."

"Sounds like the mission for a social worker, not Black Ops," said the judge with frustration.

"Sir, with all due respect, this is not social work, this isn't a help out a friend mission, and this is not something that I take lightly," said Tyler. "I understand the risks and the ramifications of selecting the wrong person and I have done that once before, and I am sure you are well aware that I eliminated that loose end when it needed to be taken care of."

"Nobody is doubting your ability or your loyalty, Tyler," said the voice. "Actually, that's the thing I'm worried about. You're loyal to this friend. You've seen his great abilities, but what I wonder about is if the vision of your youth is reality or something that you just wish he was like. Sometimes when we're young and in the heat of battle, we created an image for people around us that they couldn't possibly live up to."

"Sir, if you'll indulge me just for a moment, I'd like to tell you a little story about Michael Falau?" asked Tyler.

"Go right ahead, because at this point, I'm really feeling like we have to rescind the offer," said the voice of the judge at the other end of the phone.

"Michael Falau was a man, and is a man, that is willing to risk his life for what he thinks is right and what he believes in. I saw the glint in his eye as I told him about what we did and how we make things right, he even questioned me about if we killed people, and when I told him sometimes that needed to happen, he didn't bat an eye."

Taking a deep breath, Tyler focused in on what exactly it would take to help the judge see what he saw in his long time friend.

"Sir, the biggest part of Michael Falau is that he fights to the end. In an almost insane way, he has no regard for himself. He places the regard of his mission and the people around him above everything," said Tyler, feeling his eyes slightly start to well with tears. "He and I had been placed on a mission years ago, and we had been dropped into a hot spot where we knew the people that we needed to save were surrounded. The problem we had was we got dropped out of the helicopter in the wrong location, we had repelled down, but we didn't get the latest intel saying that the enemy had moved up and fortified its position. It was in Ukraine where we were trying to move a group of insurgents that were terrorizing the people of the town and creating their own organized crime underworld. When we got caught behind their fighting, they quickly closed in on us. It wasn't like a whole battalion or a massive number of men, but it was easily fifty. They flanked us to both sides and then pulled in around behind us. It was simply a shooting gallery. They didn't even care about the fact that they could shoot straight across and kill men in their own platoon, they were desperate to remove us, because they thought we were somehow connected with the Russian Secret Service."

"That's a tough spot to be in," said the voice, looking to add something to the conversation, but knowing he couldn't.

"I just assumed at that point we were going to die, the men started moving in slowly but of course, that's when Falau came to life, he was gonna get the hell out of there or die trying. He did something that I've never seen anybody do before, and I'll probably never see it again. We sat behind a car, shading ourselves from the fire that had been coming in from one side, it was at that point, when nothing felt like it was going to work, that Falau opened the gas cap, ripped a piece of his own shirt off and lit it on fire. Jumping into the car, he told me to cover myself in the doorway. Then he jammed the car into neutral and let the emergency brake go, and as the car started to roll down the street, the flame started to dart inside the vehicle and eventually exploded the car as it rolled away."

"He made himself a Molotov cocktail?" asked the voice.

"That's exactly what he did. He basically became a suicide bomber. He was using the car to blow a hole in their defenses, giving us a chance to run. But I wasn't aware that that's what he was doing," said Tyler. "So I was hung up in the doorway and I had taken a round in my left calf that wasn't allowing me to make a run for it when I had the opportunity. I could see the men around me, they were closing in, I gave out just short bursts of cover fire, to try to keep them at bay, but at that point, I was sure I was dead, and I was sure that Falau was dead in the car. By the time the men were within twenty-five feet of me, and just sitting on the other sides of the road, I'd all but given up, I had hardly any rounds left, and they were fully stocked. There was no backup that was gonna come for me."

"So what did Falau do?" asked the voice on the other end of the phone. "He's still alive, so he must have done something to get you out of there."

"He sure did. From what he told me later on, he had rolled himself out of the car when it exploded, he caught some burns and some shrapnel in his back and in his right leg, but he had also taken out seven of the enemy at the same time. During the confusion of the explosion he broke the window of a car sitting on the side of the road, popped in and hot-wired it. Instead of racing up the road, getting himself to freedom, and keeping himself alive, he banged a U-turn in the middle of the street, driving back into the heat and knocked down a number of the men that were ready to kill me. He used the car like a battering ram until he finally moved up to the point where I could make a run of just ten yards to get into the car. I dove through the window like I was in a superhero movie."

"And then he punched the gas and got you out of there, didn't he?" said the judge. "He saved your ass when he could've just have saved his own. He put his life on the line more than once to get you out of there."

"Not only that Your Honor, he also insisted that we finish the mission. The normal, safe thing to do in that situation would have been for us to find a place to hide out, but he kept going, and he said that if we weren't dead, we needed to move forward. I've never seen anything like it."

"And you think this is still inside him?" asked the judge. "Do you think you could bring this back out, and put this man back at that level, despite the years of drinking and despite the trouble that he's found himself in? That memory of the girl, it haunts him, and the only thing that's gonna make him better is to get rid of it."

"I think that's what this will do. He'll be back where he succeeds. He'll be back where he does what he does best," said Tyler. "He's a winner, he just doesn't remember it at this point."

"Well for your sake, I hope he is. I hope he can do everything you say, because he could be an invaluable asset that makes this organization stronger than it was before," said the voice.

"That's my hope, Sir, but as I told you before, the System is my number one priority and I won't let anything get in the way of that," said Tyler. "I can assure you, if this situation does not work out, it will be me, and me alone, that takes care of the situation. The work that we do around the world can't be jeopardized for one man or a friendship that I have."

"I admire your thinking on this, Tyler. At one time I had been placed in a similar situation, and the results weren't good," said the voice at the other end of the phone. "I just hope the results are different for you, this sounds like a man that has a tremendous amount of ability, and maybe we're the people that can help him show that and help him get to a better place in life."

FIVE

THE WINDOW at the far end of the apartment was pulled open. Falau sat on the edge of the window ledge looking down at the street, wishing he had just stayed on the steps drinking with Grady. From a tall glass, filled with whiskey, he took a long sip. As day turned into night he could see ambulances rushing up the street, with police cars soon to follow. He could hear the sounds of couples arguing in the apartments around him, often followed by the sound of something smashing due to someone's anger. A drunk stumbled up the street talking to himself. Falau wondered if this was all his future held for him.

Downing the rest of the whiskey, he pulled down the window to lock out the outside world. He stumbled into the bathroom, half filled with whiskey and half filled with disappointment at what his life had become. Staring into the mirror he saw a man that was very unhappy. A man that saw no future for himself. A man he did not like. Swinging the medicine cabinet open he reached for some of the sleeping pills that had become an all too common feature of his life.

They were the one and only thing he could ever count on to help shut out the flashbacks and nightmares that were his tortured past. Well, that, and mixing them with booze. Even then the combination only stopped the invaders of his mind some of the time. Popping off the top of the bottle, he could see there were just a few pills left, maybe just five or six. Dumping them all into his hand, he stumbled back out of the bathroom. Slumping down on his bed, he grabbed the half finished bottle of whiskey and threw the pills into his mouth. Taking a long hard slug from the bottle he swilled them down into his stomach. He wasn't sure if that amount of pills was even safe to take, but at this point he didn't care. He took one last hard drag off the bottle, feeling the rush to his head. Placing the bottle on the floor he fell back onto the bed and stared at the ceiling.

"Just one night. Just one night without the dreams. Is that too much to ask?" barked Falau looking to the ceiling.

Feeling the pills starting to overtake him, his eyes rolled up into the back of his head and he let himself slip into a light sleep where he bounced between reality and dreams. The place the nightmares came from.

With the promise of sleep on its way, the sound of an ambulance rushing down the street and its screaming siren broke through his potential slumber. The sirens echoed off the brownstones that covered each side of the street creating a cacophony of sound that turned all heads nearby. Trying to open his eyes, he couldn't fight the force of the pills now digging deep into his mind and forcing the sleep to come, despite the distraction of the ambulance.

Deep in the back of his consciousness he slipped into a state caught somewhere between asleep and awake. From there he could hear the scream of a woman and he desperately wanted to help her. The nightmare was coming on strong and there was no way it could be stopped. He felt like he was watching a movie but he was also somehow in the movie. The vision of dark hair zipped across his eyes and he saw the bloodstained mask of a woman's face crossing his field of vision. He thrashed side to side in his bed to try and wake up, but it was no use. He was now stuck in the world where people try to control their dreams and change what's going on. But Falau knew that could never happen. Like every other night before this, it was something he simply needed to endure. It was the worst kind of nightmare, the one where he could think. The ones that he just watched were so much easier. He would just have to go through the torture and come out the other side. In these nightmares, he knew he was simply being tortured, his mind forcing him to see the cold, hard images over and over again.

As he slipped deeper into the dream he found himself in the car again. In the passenger seat was a beautiful woman with dark hair that fell down over her shoulders. She shifted in her seat so her back was against the door and she smiled at him, intently, with love deep in her eyes. She was everything he'd ever wanted... smart, funny, beautiful, and above all, intelligent. She was the classic girl next door. She would fall in love with him, and he had never felt so lucky.

He approached and stopped at the red light, looking over to her, she smiling at him. Feeling the loving closeness there, filled him with undeniable joy.

Without warning he was suddenly in the intersection, looking over the beautiful woman's shoulder, through the window, at the oncoming truck speeding hard toward them, the logo on the front of the grill getting closer and closer. Flecks of white paint all over the front bumper and dirt that had not been washed off in some time. The metallic green of the hood racing closer and closer. Opening his mouth, nothing but silence came out. He needed to warn her, he needed to let her know, but there was nothing but silence. The truck slammed into the passenger side door, crushing the side of the car and forcing the woman to catapult forward. The smile disappeared from the woman's face as her body lurched and snapped with the powerful impact of the collision.

She flew through the air, crashing her face hard into the steering wheel, her hair wrapped around the wheel, the sudden impact causing her head to stop viciously.

His eyes and head snapped up to the ceiling of the car in an uncontrollable force of power from the crash. He was no longer able to control his head or which direction his body traveled. He lost sight of the beautiful woman for just a moment. Pulling his eyes down and looking back to her, he could see she had started to recoil and she was falling back off the steering wheel into view. A deep rip cut down the center of her face. The cut ran from her forehead, through her eyebrows, over her nose, and down her left cheek, and it was filling with blood. Her crushed nose had moved out of position. Her eyes had lost all their sparkle. She stared blankly into the air. She was conscious and she was looking directly at him as if asking him for help. But there was nothing he could do for her. He wanted to reach out for her. He wanted to help her. He wanted to save her from what was about to happen next. But he couldn't. It was beyond his control.

Falau felt his head snap forward again, causing a great pain to shoot up from his neck and into his back. His hands bounced off the steering wheel, causing the airbag to deploy and force its way into his face. Just as this happened he reached out for the woman, who was incapable of reaching back. Now going hard backwards her head slammed through the broken window. Her body bent and lifted out through the passenger window, hitting the pickup truck before recoiling again and being forced back into the car. As the airbag started to deflate, he opened his eyes to see her covered with glass. She had fallen into the well of the passenger seat. Her head tilted back as her body had crumbled. Her eyes were open but there was no life. Falau reached out to her, still fighting the airbag, trying to get closer. Shards of glass were embedded deep into her face, causing her to look as if she was wearing a mask. As the airbag deflated he grabbed her hand, shaking it and screaming to her, but there was no response. As he screamed for help he jolted himself out of the drug and alcohol fueled sleep, finally saving him from his nightmare from hell. Breathing hard, his chest sent strong pains shooting down his left arm. Falau's eyes stared at the ceiling and his fists clenched hard as he took several deep breaths, trying to control his emotions.

"No!" he shouted as he turned and his fist pounded the mattress. Reaching to the side, he grabbed the bottle of whiskey and threw it at the wall, shattering it, and spilling the contents, leaving him alone with his thoughts. Looking up to the ceiling, tears started to fill his eyes as Falau said, "I'm sorry."

SIX

THE SOUND of the skill saw filled the air and muted the sounds of the hammers crashing down on the nails they were driving home, and the occasional shouts of men moving around the worksite trying to get their jobs done before the end of the day.

"Fuck!" exclaimed Falau, hitting his thumb with a hammer as he started to frame a wall.

"You'd think by now you'd have that down," joked a large man wearing a hard hat. "Who let you have a hammer anyways? I thought you were a laborer."

"I am, but they were short of carpenters so they gave me something easy to do."

"Their mistake. Next thing you know you'll be in line for some injury pay."

Falau laughed with the man but kept about his work. He was more than happy to be building a wall rather than lugging bricks or shingles, like you would normally do as a laborer. As the day grew longer three o'clock hit and all the union members called it a day. There was no such luck for

Falau and the other non-union men. They would work until dark and for less pay.

"Falau, I can't believe you're doing a job like this," said the older man with graying hair on his temples and a hardened weathered look on his face.

"What do you mean, Gino?" asked Falau, not lifting his head from the cleaning of the floor that he had become accustomed to doing each and every afternoon.

"I mean, what are you doing here, man? You're not like the rest of us. You should be out doing something big with your life," said Gino keeping about his business as well, and not to draw the ire of a foreman.

"Oh, I'm just a guy like you," said Falau. "I put my pants on one leg at a time and I always remember to close the door when I leave the house. You can't ask for much more from me than that."

"Oh, sure, Falau, that's what you say all the time, pushing everything off with a joke," said Gino, lifting his head and staring directly at Falau. The younger man could feel the gaze of his friend hard upon him. It was a typical reaction that he had gotten almost everywhere he had been. Someone would sniff out that he was overqualified for the job he was doing and then confront him on why he was settling for a job that he was overqualified to do.

"Gino, I like life simple, it's not a big thing. I'm just not one of those guys that goes out and tries to charge up the corporate ladder," said Falau, still continuing not to make eye contact with the man.

"You're lying to me, Falau," said Gino, letting a small snicker come out at the end of the sentence. "Every time you lie to me, you won't look at me. I know you're a hard worker, but you're not that hard a worker."

Falau let off a laugh trying to divert the attention away from the original question that the man had asked.

"Come on, man, tell me, what's your story, what's your background all about," said Gino, putting his broom under his right forearm and leaning against the wall.

"I told you before, I'm just a regular guy. I grew up on the South Shore and I've pretty much stuck here ever since," said Falau, looking up at Gino quickly and dismissing his question as if it had nothing to do with his life.

"So you're telling me that a guy like you, who's clearly well-educated. For God's sakes, you read a book at lunch. You see any other guy around here reading books during lunch?" asked Gino. "You look like a damn movie star, you got that chiseled jaw tough look and you're always able to figure out every problem we have around here and get a solution for it."

"I'm a mechanical guy. What can I say?" said Falau. "It's just in my nature. Things make sense when it comes to construction."

"Oh come on, man, the other day, you were reading a book by Nietzsche," said Gino laughing hard and pointing to the backpack of Falau's that sat in the far corner of the room. "Do you realize we had probably six different ways to pronounce that guy's name? We couldn't even figure it out. We had to go ask."

"Now I could have helped with that," said Falau as he laughed at the picture in his mind's eyes of his friends and co-workers trying to figure out why he would be reading such a text.

"Well, we're not that dumb, we did know that that guy was a philosopher from way back when. But not one of us could figure out a time that we ever read a book about philosophy," said Gino, adding a robust laugh to that of Falau's.

"What can I say? I've always enjoyed that kind of stuff. I always liked the idea of what's going on inside us."

"Which leads me back to my question, what are you doing here?" asked Gino. "I already told you, we know you're smart and we know you're a great looking guy and we know that you're as loyal as all get out. So why is a guy with all that going for him in here doing non-union labor work? We all know you're too good for this. You had to have had some opportunities somewhere along the line."

"College and all that just never really interested me. I was good in school, I did a good job, but nothing ever really set me on fire, so I never got into anything," said Falau, hoping that the lie would sound convincing. "I did spend a couple of years in the military, but even that became a bit much for me."

"You mean to tell me in that big giant army, they couldn't find one thing that you liked. For God's sake, they made a movie about one of those guys being on the radio," said Gino. "You can do anything in the army. They'll train you to do everything in the world, anything from digging a latrine to becoming a doctor."

"I guess I just let that one go by, kinda screwed up."

"I'm not buying it Falau, I think you're full of crap," said Gino, moving over and placing his arm around the shoulder of Falau. "You're a special person. You're one of those guys that's got it all going for you and you know you got it going on. So the big question is, why aren't you taking charge of it? And I'm not buying that it's just 'cause you didn't feel like it."

"I don't know Gino. What do I have to do to convince you? You obviously think that I'm trying to hold something back on you. But I promise you friend, I'm not," said Falau, looking over Gino's shoulder Falau spotting the foreman coming down the hall.

"Straighten up, it's the boss," said Falau quickly.

Gino quickly pulled his broom and slid into the adjoining room keeping himself out of sight from the boss.

"Hey Falau, get over here," called a short man wearing jeans and a t-shirt, also wearing a hard hat.

"Ya, boss. What's up?"

"You're fired, that's what's up," said the little man without looking up from his clipboard.

"What?" questioned Falau.

"You heard me, you're fired. Nothing can be done about it. We need to cut back," insisted the boss. Dodging the issue with Falau he called to another worker, telling him to get back to work.

"Is it something I did wrong? Did I not work hard enough?"

The little man raised his head from his clipboard letting out a long and exaggerated sigh. "Falau, it's simple. You were the last hired and now you're the first fired. That's the way it goes with construction. It's nothing personal. Just economics."

Falau stood staring into space as his newly ex-boss walked away without so much as saying goodbye. Falau walked over, grabbed his toolbelt and left the final prospect of employment he had.

WALKING up the steps to his apartment, Falau held a pint of whiskey in his right hand. The bottle was already open and half the contents were inside Falau.

I bet the rich people don't have to climb stairs, he thought, urging his legs to climb one more step and then one more after that.

Turning down the hallway, he could see an envelope taped to the door of his apartment. Falau sighed, knowing nobody ever left good news in an envelope taped to the door of your apartment. Snatching it hard from the door he dug his fingers into the seal and opened it. Swaying where he stood, he shook open the paper and started to read:

Dear Mr. Falau,
We've attempted to reach you no less than two dozen times over the last two months. Each time we have been unable to contact you. We have also been made aware that you have changed the locks on your apartment. This is in clear violation of your tenant agreement.
More alarming than this is the fact that you've not paid rent in over three months. By not returning our attempted contacts to you, and the lack of payment, you leave us no choice but to evict you from your apartment. You have one week in which to remove all your things and move out. If you do not comply, the local sheriff will be contacted to force your removal.
All the best,
Arthur Steinberg

FALAU'S HEAD shook as he finished the letter. Having no money and no job, he crumpled the letter in his hand and threw it on the floor. Taking another long sip from the bottle, he fished in his pocket for the keys to unlock the door. Unsteady on his feet, he bumped into the door frame as his key slipped into the lock and he pushed the door open.

"Home sweet home," he mumbled to himself, taking another sip from the bottle, slamming the door closed with a kick. "I wonder if old Mr. Steinberg would ever have the courage to come over here and ask me for the rent himself?"

Staggering across the room, Falau dropped himself onto the sofa, causing the covering sheet to fall off. Resting his head back on the sofa, he felt the internal foam against his head. Reaching behind him, he could feel the exposed internal springs of the sofa pressing against his head.

"I can't even afford a real sofa," complained Falau to nobody but himself, his words slurred. Taking a handful of the foam, he ripped it from the sofa and threw it down on the floor. "Not even a decent sofa. How can a man my age not have decent furniture? I'm such a loser, I can't even afford to get a sofa that doesn't have holes in it!"

Without warning, a flash of the bloodied face, of the woman he loved, falling back across the car after the impact of the crash, passed before his eyes, the sound of the voice calling out, "You did it... it's your fault", echoing in his mind.

"Bullshit!" snapped Falau. "You're the one doing it to me. You're trying to kill me. Can't you just let me go and let me move on with my life?"

Shaking his head, he attempted to remove the horror from his mind but it would not let go. The image of the pickup, crashing into the passenger side of the car, replayed over and over again in his head. One impact after another. The metal and glass breaking. The look crossing the face of the woman as her body absorbed the impact of the collision.

Fighting the flashback, Falau downed the rest of the whiskey. Drinking himself into unconsciousness was one of the only things he felt he could do in times like this. The bottle fell to the floor as the whiskey hit him hard. His head dropping back, he caught sight of the exposed pipes running across the ceiling in his apartment.

Slurring his words he mumbled, "...couldn't even give me a decent ceiling. Exposed pipes. A slum..."

Falau's eyes did not leave the pipes. Examining them, he felt by the thickness of them they were strong and sturdy, a lot like the ones he helped install on a construction job downtown.

Falau pulled his drunk self-up, walked over to the table at the far end of the room, took the chair that sat behind it. Dragging the chair and shaking it as he went, he tested it for strength.

"Yeah, that'll hold me."

Drunk with a pint of whiskey inside him, he gingerly pulled himself onto the chair in the standing position. The chair quivered and he waited for it to shoot out from under him if he put too much weight to any one side.

Placing his hands above his head, Falau reached up and grabbed the pipe. Slowly placing his weight on it, he felt the pipe move downward in the holes cut at either end of the room. Falau lifted his feet off the chair and started to swing. A smile crossed his face as he hung from the pipe. As soon as the smile appeared, it disappeared just as quick, as he realized the pipe would hold his weight after all.

Dropping his feet back to the chair, he regained his balance and looked up at the pipe again. His hands dropped and he unbuckled the belt from his pants. The belt was leather and strong, with slight wear marks. Falau had gotten it at the Salvation Army and he knew it was in better shape than anything he owned. He pulled the belt in his hands, feeling how strong it was, before he reached up and fed it over the pipe. He took the leather, fed it through the buckle, and clasped it.

Grabbing the belt with two hands, he pulled down hard on it. "If I jump hard that should do it," he said, in a matter-of-fact tone.

Inching his way closer to the edge of the chair, Falau pulled the belt tighter and toward him. Leaning forward, he got his head close to the belt and attempted to slide it through the loop.

"Lord forgive me," he whispered.

Before he could get the belt around his neck, his weight shifted the chair and it shot out from under him. Momentarily he felt he was hanging in the air and that the belt would snap his neck, causing all the pain to stop. But his body dropped, and he could see the belt hanging from the pipe as he fell to the ground, crashing off the coffee table and breaking it in half under the weight of his large and powerful body.

Falau felt pain shoot across his back, from the impact on the table, as he lay on the floor looking back up at the pipe. Raising one hand up into the air as if to grab the belt again, Falau moaned in pain, as much emotional as physical.

"Constant failure," Falau said, reflecting on himself and all that he was not.

Rolling over, he got to his hands and knees and started to stand up. Pushing the rubble of the broken coffee table aside, he saw the business card Tyler had given him among the broken pieces.

Reaching down to pick it up, he inspected the number. Nodding his head, he started to laugh.

"You got me, Ty."

SEVEN

THE BLACK FOUR-DOOR Mercedes pulled up, screeching to a halt in front of the building. Falau sat on the steps, looking over, as he saw the passenger window come down.

"Let's go," said Tyler, leaning across the passenger side seat and pushing open the door.

Falau made his way across the sidewalk and hopped into the waiting car. All eyes in the neighborhood were watching to see exactly what their neighbor was up to. Before fully swinging the door shut, Tyler screeched away from the sidewalk and was on his way down Massachusetts Avenue. Shifting his eyes to the dash, Falau could see Tyler had the car going 60 miles an hour, on a main road, on the streets of Boston, at two o'clock in the afternoon.

"Nice power. What's the rush?" asked Falau.

"No rush at all. Don't worry about it, I have it under control," replied Tyler as he smiled over at his long-time friend.

Tyler proceeded to weave in and out of cars, pulling over at random spots, and pulling in and out of parking lots, as if it was all a normal thing to do. The constant screeching of tires and jamming of brakes made Falau feel nauseous.

"You caught on yet?" asked Tyler.

"Yeah, I think I've figured it out. You're checking to see if anyone's tailing us."

"You learn fast. It's good to have you on the team," Tyler replied, gripping the wheel tight as the Mercedes dug into another sharp corner. "I love that you called. Does this mean you're ready to join us on a mission?"

Falau fidgeted in his seat and leaned his head back slightly on the head rest. "Yeah, I'm ready," said the big man.

"That's good. I have one for you. It's middle-of-the-road for the kind of work we do, but I think it's a good one to get your feet wet on," said Tyler, shifting the car again abruptly to the side.

"Instead of driving like this, wouldn't it be easier just to try to blend in with everybody else?" asked Falau with a smirk, as he grabbed the dashboard around a tight corner.

Reaching out, Tyler shook Falau's hand. "Welcome aboard." Releasing his grip, he leaned forward and opened the glove compartment, pulling out a small envelope. Giving the envelope to Falau he continued to move in and out of the traffic.

"This is just some walking around money. You'll need it for where you're going. It can get pretty expensive there."

Opening the envelope exposed thousands of dollars in different currencies. He quickly slid it into his jacket and out of sight. "That will come in handy," said Falau, wondering if what he had said was true.

"Okay, let me make one thing clear to you right now. Nobody knows who we are. Nobody knows what we do.

Because of that, everything is far more complicated. This means that you're going to be watched by different people. Just like I am watched by people every single day. The inside word is that they think I'm part of an international drug running cartel, so they have me on constant surveillance, exactly what the judges want. Doesn't matter what country I go to, their Secret Service is always right on me. I let them follow me and I let them see what I'm doing until I don't want them to follow me and don't want them to see what I'm doing. This keeps their eyes on me and not on the judges or the system that we've built. I'm the guy they focus on, the guy that they come after," explained Tyler with all the seriousness he could muster.

"Seems like a lot to take on, more than any one guy should have to."

"It's really not that bad. I'm just giving these guys the slip sometimes and then helping them catch up at other times. They're just doing their jobs, and they never can find anything because I never do anything that they're looking for. They just keep trying to get close to me and figure out what I'm up to."

Holding the wheel hard, he ripped into a parking garage, not stopping for a ticket. He raced down to the end of the aisle, cutting hard to the right to go down another level. Reaching the bottom floor, screeches echoed off the wall as his tires dug hard into each turn, the sound bouncing back off the walls like kids screaming into the Grand Canyon.

"All this just for me?" quipped Falau as they came to a stop in the parking spot with a large garage door in front of it.

Tyler jumped out of the car, went over to an access panel and entered a code, before waving his friend over. Falau got out of the car, careful not to move too close. He didn't want to give Tyler any reason to think that he was looking at the code. Hearing a loud clicking noise, Tyler walked over, grabbed the bottom of the door, and pulled the garage door up to reveal a large area for his car.

Falau caught up to Tyler inside the garage. Turning around, Tyler pulled the garage door closed and jammed on the lock.

"You leave your car there?"

Tyler laughed turning to his old friend. "The door is not to keep my car in, it's to keep everybody else out. This is not your ordinary garage."

Tyler pushed the tool rack aside to reveal the trapdoor in the floor. Popping the door up, he flipped a switch to turn the lights on. Then he went down a ladder about ten-feet to a dirt floor that was small and cramped. Without hesitation Falau worked his way down the ladder. On the dirt floor, the two men had to crouch low to make their way into a tunnel that was no larger than four-feet tall and two-feet wide. The reason for the size of the tunnel was obvious to Falau; It would deter anyone who made their way into it. This was the kind of place that someone could easily get stuck, and it would cost them their life, not being able to find their way out. As they moved along there were various turns and offshoots that would confuse anybody that had entered the system of catacombs. Tyler wove his way in and out to the amazement of Falau. He knew it all too well and made no hesitation taking turns or doubling back at any time. He had clearly run this course hundreds of times before.

Reaching a ladder, he turned back to his old friend. "This is it. Only go through the door if you're fully with us. You will see things and learn things that nobody else knows. And for everything that goes along with that, there is a price. This is no summer camp, and you're not allowed to just walk away. I vouched for you. I told them who you were, and they trusted me. I hope that I can trust you."

Falau smiled, showing Tyler he had nothing to worry about. "I'm ready to take this on. Who knows, maybe it's a second career..."

Tyler patted the back of his old friend and climbed the ladder. Tyler knocked on the door in a rhythmic pattern that resembled a jazz tune. The door slid open and the two men climbed up and into the room.

Falau didn't dare wipe the dust off his body in the beautiful room, with hardwood floors, a large oak desk, some leather clad furniture, and walls lined with books. He smiled, realizing the room probably cost more than everything he had ever owned in his entire life.

Tyler straightened his jacket and walked over to a bar adorned with decanters filled with numerous spirits. "You want a drink?"

Before Falau could respond a voice boomed out from above. "He doesn't need a drink," said the mysterious voice of a man that had been altered with electronics.

Tyler turned to Falau with a smile and a drink in his hand. "They don't trust you. At least not yet."

A look of frustration settled over Falau and his hands balled up into fists. "There needs to be some kind of trust for us to do this kind of work. I can't just go on any mission you want me to. Trust is a two-way street, and I need to know there's some from you."

Again, the voice from above boomed out, "You want to leave, or do you want to stay?"

Falau stood silent, looking up at the ceiling. Frustrated by being unable to speak to anyone, he started to pace the room.

The voice spoke out again. "Mr. Falau, this group and the System will live on, with or without you. We do not need you. It is my understanding that you can help us with our work and that you're willing to do some for us. But please understand you're doing us no favors. We have let you get this far because we think that you're capable of doing good. It's totally up to you whether you choose to go forward with this or not. But I need a commitment one way or the other, right here, right now. You can let your pride get the best of you, or you can do something meaningful with your life. It's totally up to you."

Falau stopped pacing and sat down on the couch, looking directly up at the ceiling. "It's just that I feel stupid talking to the ceiling," he said in a sarcastic tone. "You have to admit it's a little bit silly."

"I can understand your feelings about this, but you must note that all contact is with Tyler only. This is his mission and that is what he does. It helps us keep the System in order. Too many people knowing too many things leads to too many problems."

Nodding his head in agreement, Falau could fully understand what he was talking about. But he still wanted to know who the man he was going to work for really was. The voice spoke again, this time in a calmer, more relaxed tone, "At the end of each mission you can choose whether you wish to be in or out going forward. All we ask is that you never say anything about what you do. I can tell you that no person who has ever been a member of this team has ever left, and no one has ever opted out."

Walking in front of Falau, Tyler took a sip of his

beverage. "You see Falau, the mission here is to bring people back for justice. Just like I told you before. But we would never be able to do this without keeping contact to a minimum. You're going to be one of many guys and women who do this kind of work in different corners of the world."

Falau smiled and crossed his arms in front of his chest. "And maybe kill people."

"Who said anything about that?" said Tyler, his tone now one of anger before the great voice in the ceiling intervened again.

"Sometimes we need to kill someone. It is the ugly part of what we do. Nobody likes it. If we do kill someone it is in the face of overwhelming evidence. Just to put your mind at ease, people that have been hurt by the System are clearly people who have done great damage."

"Justice takes on many forms," agreed Falau.

"Yes, it does," said the voice.

Tyler walked across the room to the desk set against the wall and removed a file from the top drawer. Bringing the file over, he opened it and handed it to Falau. At first glance he could see the face of a hardened man of South American descent. He had a long scar running down his left cheek and eyes that looked as if they'd witnessed a lifetime of fighting.

At first, he simply flipped through the file. "You have one chance to look at it and then it gets put away. My advice is to commit as much of it to memory as possible," said Tyler sitting down on the couch next to his friend.

The voice from above spoke again. "As you can see, the target is Raul Mallarino, in Colombia, South America. He is a known drug smuggler. He is responsible for killing hundreds of thousands of people who used heroin cut with carfentanil. We don't typically go after drug smugglers, but this particular one clearly understood that using the carfentanil would result in the deaths of many people. We also have clear information that he himself—and his crew—are responsible for adding carfentanil to the drugs before they come into the United States. He buys from the main growers and suppliers in the local area. Then he cuts it, increases his profit, and sells it out of Miami and some European cities. The addicts don't care that so many people die from it. They think they can just use less to get high."

"What is this carfentanil shit?"

"In short it is a death sentence, most of the time," the voice from above called out. "Some people call it elephant heroin. It is ten-thousand times stronger than morphine. When this junk is found in drug supplies they call in hazmat teams to deal with it because it can be absorbed through the skin. Normally Narcan is the thing that keeps opioid overdosers alive, but with carfentanil it hardly works at all. The doctors have to use large doses of Narcan if they even get to see the patient in time. This stuff is a killing machine."

Falau read through the pages, taking in as much information as possible. "My God, this guy is sick. The beheadings, mutilations, attacks on families, killing children and the elderly. Seems like there is nothing this guy won't do."

Tyler shifted and turned toward his friend. "They call him El Carnicero, which translates into The Butcher. It was a nickname that he picked up from the local police down in Columbia. They called him that because when they went to the scenes after his attacks, the men said it looked a lot like a butcher's shop after they'd just dissected an animal. There was always blood and body parts everywhere. This guy knows how to send a message to everybody in the community, and all his competitors. You're going to buy from just him, or you are going to die."

"The worst part is that he had been captured and held. The United States demanded him to be extradited from Colombia, but they refused to send him. Power of the drug cartels got to too many people on the inside, and they threatened their families if they didn't keep The Butcher from being sent to the States. So now he is back on the street doing what he has always done without any punishment at all. At this point he feels unstoppable, now he has this kind of backing," said the voice from above.

"The judges want this guy alive. They want to see what he has to say and then figure out what should be done," stated Tyler.

"Do you realize what you're asking me? You act like it's no big deal! You want me to go in and infiltrate a drug smuggling operation and then bring the guy back to the United States alive. Oh, and the guy's called The Butcher! The man is a horrific murderer, and you just want me to grab him and pop him on a plane and fly back here to the States? Maybe while I'm at it you should have me capture a unicorn. Anything else that's completely impossible you want me to do?"

"We will give you your full choice of your own supplies, and Tyler can help. You know what he can produce for you. Maybe a few gadgets that can help you out."

Shaking his head back and forth, Falau looked over at Tyler as if to say, 'this is all crazy'.

"Mr. Falau, the time to answer is now. Are you in or are you out?"

EIGHT

SITTING on board the 747 flying at thirty-five-thousand-feet, Falau's fingers turned white as he gripped tightly to the armrest. For a man who didn't enjoy flying in the slightest, sitting in coach packed amongst the travelers, the smells of their bodies, and their crying kids was almost too unbearable. To make all that worse, he was wedged in the middle seat, with a man to his left he was sure was trying to break the record for loudest snoring, and to his right an overweight gentleman in an oversized cowboy hat. The fat man's belly hung over the armrest, not allowing any room for Falau to put his arm down. He spent the whole flight with one hand on his lap and the other one holding the armrest tight, each set of turbulence causing him to gasp and sweat even harder.

"Hello ladies and gentlemen, this is your captain John Sterling speaking. As you may have felt by now, we're hitting some turbulence, but that's to be expected. If you can all try and stay in your seats most of the flight, we can avoid any injuries resulting from more unexpected turbulence.

There is no need to put on your seatbelt at this time, so try to sit back and enjoy the flight."

But as soon as the captain's voice stopped then another abrupt bout of turbulence hit the plane, jostling it from side to side. Falau shook in the seat and bumped against the fat man's body. His breath quickened and he gasped for air, alerting those around him to his nervousness and stress.

"You okay, Hoss?" asked the fat man in the cowboy hat. A soothing drawl rolled in his speech as if he wasn't even aware of the turbulence.

"Yeah. Just a bad flyer. Never been very good at this at all."

The fat man reached out his hand for Falau to shake it and introduced himself as Billy Ray Johnson. "I'm in coffee products. I sell everything to do with them, so heading down to Columbia's nothing new for me," said Falau with a southern accent. More turbulence rocked the plane hard, pushing him hard into the cowboy's belly. Realizing that he had been holding the man's hand for far too long, he quickly removed it.

"Hey buddy don't worry about it, this happens to a lot of people. I fly this route all the time and its constant turbulence. We will be okay, don't worry about that."

"I don't understand planes. It seems to defy all logic and physics to me. No matter how many times people tell me how it works, it just doesn't make sense," said Falau, trying to get a small laugh from Billy.

With great effort, Billy wiggled his way out of his seat and stood up in the aisle. Leaning into Falau, he reached into his coat pocket he pulled out what appeared to be a small MP3 player and some headphones. "Maybe you should listen to this. I think it will help you a lot."

The cowboy made his way to the back of the plane and out of sight of Falau, who was left holding the gift. Again, the turbulence hit, but in a twist the aircraft moved up and down rather than side to side. Falau felt himself completely raise out of the seat and hit down hard. In an act of desperation, his hands fumbled around the headphones and he shoved them on his head. At this point he was willing to do anything to try to make the flight easier on his stress levels. As the sweat ran down his temples, the sound of classical music started. The smooth sound of the piano and gentle violins played in Falau's ears, and he was sure that Billy knew exactly what he was talking about, as he immediately started to relax.

As the music played, Falau felt himself dipping into sleep. Tyler's voice gently entered his ears as if he was a DJ announcing the next song with the music behind him.

"Hey there, friend. I see that you've met my cowboy buddy. He's a good guy. Knowing how hard flying was for you, he gave you this gift." Tyler's voice fell quite over the next few seconds but the beautiful music playing had Falau picturing Tyler in his mind's eyes, though he could still feel himself falling into a deeper sleep. This was no doubt one of Tyler's inventions that he'd developed just for Falau on this flight.

"This message can only be listened to once, and then never again. It will self-erase. Falau, you're going to meet with a contact. The name of the contact is Vick, and when the time is right Vick will contact you, and it will be unmistakable."

Falau could feel himself drifting into a deeper and deeper sleep but still was able to retain everything Tyler was saying. The mad genius still had all the skills Falau had known from long before. He could create and develop things, that no one else could, in an incredibly short amount of time. Tyler's words were embedding deep into his mind without Falau making any effort to make it happen.

"At this point, and we must make some of this quick, sleep should start setting in and you won't be waking up until you're close to the airport. I have a couple of fun things that you might enjoy on your mission," said Tyler with obvious enthusiasm dripping from every word. He seemed unable to contain himself from what he was about to tell Falau. "So, we set you up with clothing to wear on your flight down there. Of course, the clothing isn't going to be just normal clothing. The belt you have on, the leather jacket, the collar on your shirt, are all things that can help you. First off, your belt. It's really a very simple design. It's a homing beacon. If at any time you get distressed, to the point where you can't get out and you need some back up, squeeze the belt buckle as hard as you can. It will start a reaction that will deploy people to your location and help you get out of there as fast as possible. I warn you to only use this in the most extreme of circumstances, as it will blow our cover. There's no way that you can activate the homing beacon and expect we could ever go back and attempt to pick up a target after this has been done. The next wonderful little thing you have is the leather jacket you have on. It's bulletproof. I know you're thinking that it fits well and it's comfortable and flexible, probably even the best jacket you've ever owned. What's more, if someone fired an M-16 at you from close range, all you would suffer is a bad bruise on your body. The bullet would not get through in any way. Granted that will not protect your head if they should hit you there. Your brains would just splatter in an instant, so at least it would be quick.

Next the collar on your shirt. Inside the collar you'll feel something that feels like two plastic tabs. But they're not. On the right side, if you pull up the tab there is a small injection needle. This will knock anyone out for several hours. It is a one time only use device. The collar on the left side that, well that can be pulled out and used as a razor blade for combat or any other situation you might need."

Turbulence hit the plane again, jostling Falau about, but now he didn't have a care in the world. He was drifting to the sounds of music and gently riding the wave of the violence from the turbulence while listening to the soothing sound of Tyler's voice and feeling more at ease with every word his friend said.

"Your contact Vick is an insider, and is one of the best people we have. You can learn a lot. You're going to want to keep your mouth closed and take in every bit of information. Remember you're a first timer!"

All the snoring of the man next to him no longer bothered Falau, and all the turbulence seemed to no longer have any effect on him. And he felt that the best part about it was at some level he was conscious enough to understand what Tyler did for him, and all the instructions he was being given.

Tyler's voice continued, "When you land, make your way to the hotel we told you about. People will want to know what you're doing there. Columbia takes new businessman coming in very seriously. They are going to wonder what you are all about, because they keep a sharp eye out for anybody they think might be involved in the drug trade. Well it seems like you're about to fall into the deepest sleep that you've ever had in your life. You're going to wake up rested, alert, and ready to go. I have total confidence in you. I know what you can do and I know you're the right man for the job. Good night, Falau, and good luck."

Falau's eyes closed and he drifted between consciousness and deep sleep. The music continued but Tyler's voice was gone, as if it had all been a dream.

NINE

THE CAPTAIN'S voice crackled through the airplane's old public address system.

"Ladies and gentlemen, can you please return to your seats and return your tray tables into their locked and upright positions. Please also put on your seatbelt. We will be landing at El Dorado International Airport in Bogotá, Colombia, in just a few moments."

Falau saw the ground approaching quickly, and fearing somehow the aircraft would get out of control and crash to the ground was too much.

Best thing I can do is keep my eyes straightforward while the plane settles down, thought Falau.

He looked about the aircraft, trying to find the cowboy as he wanted to thank him for the gift he had given him, but Billy was nowhere to be seen, not even the massive cowboy hat. A man that large is too difficult to hide from site. How can a man that big simply disappear on an airplane at thirty-five-thousand-feet?

As the plane made its final approach the Captain came

over the public address system again. "Ladies and gentlemen, your Captain again with a few pieces of information that may come in handy to you. Bogotá currently has a temperature 65°F. There are mostly cloudy skies with sunshine peeking through. It looks like a beautiful Columbian day. We are on our final approach. Please stay in your seats and refrain from walking about the cabin for your safety. Have a good day, and thank you for flying Copa Airlines."

Within five minutes the plane touched down on the runway, Falau's heavy breathing finally calming down. The last five minutes had felt like an hour as he felt as if the plane was falling rather than landing. The touchdown of the wheels had made him jump in his seat, but also brought with it a wave of relief that he was back on terra firma.

The pilot edged the plane to the terminal and rolled to a stop. The jet way inched across and the seatbelt light turned off. At once everyone sprang from their seats, reaching up and pulling their carry-on luggage from the overhead compartments. They then all pushed and shoved to gain one spot ahead in the line of people waiting to disembark the plane. Staying in his seat, Falau always wondered why people worked so hard just to get one or two spots ahead in the line. Once out in the terminal it would make no difference, but people always needed that little victory in some way.

Falau secured his bag tightly behind his back. He was sure from Tyler's briefing that photographs would be taken of him from the moment he landed. Security would have the manifest of the plane and any outsiders would be processed through the security check list. There was no doubt that someone out there had eyes on him right now.

The photographs would upload directly into the computer system. Facial recognition would check every person that arrived on every flight, all faces checked against the database with all the security systems, both nationally and internationally. If a person had so much as a parking ticket the Colombian government would know about it in less than 5 minutes.

Fully aware that by this point they were watching him, Falau made his way off the jet way and into the terminal. Walking straight for the new arrivals customs area, a young man stepped in front of him holding out his hand.

"Sir, do you speak English?"

"Yes," said Falau.

"Sorry to stop you, but you have been randomly selected for a baggage check. I hope you understand this is standard protocol, and you are just the person that randomly came up. We have no reason to suspect you of any wrong doing. We will try to complete this as fast as possible," said the young man in uniform.

Falau rolled his eyes, keeping in disguise, playing the part of the frustrated traveler.

"I have been through this numerous times. I understand," said Falau.

Falau slid his hands in his pockets, looking at his bags and back at the officer. Giving him, 'the look' did not appear to speed anything up, despite Falau's obvious frustration. Making eye contact back with Falau, the official slowed his speed in response to the attitude of the American.

The two walked over to a table, set against a wall, just to the side of the main area. Falau placed the bag onto the table.

The official stared into the open bag. "Do you have anything to be declared?"

"No."

"Are you transporting anything that the country of Columbia would find illegal?"

"No. Not to my knowledge. Feel free to check everything if you like," Falau said, lacing his words with sarcasm and disgust.

"Sir, you do understand how long I could make this search go on for, don't you?"

"Yes, I do. Sorry. It was a long flight."

"Understood, Sir. May I have your passport?"

Looking through the passport and checking each detail, Falau was sure that if anything was slightly out of place he would be directly on a flight back to the United States.

"Your papers say you're in farming equipment. Seems like a waste of time if you ask me. We have more than enough farming supply companies here in Colombia. Who would ever want a product from the United States when you can get one here?" asked the officer, jabbing at Falau.

Falau just smiled and nodded his head. He knew exactly what the official was trying to do, but he was not going to take the bait and resisted the temptation to reply.

A higher-ranking officer walked over to them, a variety of ranking bars across the shoulders of his uniform. He looked to be in his fifties and did not make any eye contact with Falau. He leaned into the young man in the uniform and whispered in his ear, changing the expression on the young man's face.

The officer, suddenly sounding more official, stated, "Your itinerary please."

Falau reached into his jacket pocket and pulled out two pieces of paper, bound together, and handed them to the young man. He checked the papers closely and then photographed them. Handing them back, he stared at Falau.

"I hope you enjoy your stay here in Colombia. You are free to go," said the young man abruptly.

Gathering his things, he slid to the end of the table and pulled them into his arms. Walking and repacking his case at the same time, he knew that he was now on their radar and he hadn't even made it out of customs yet.

TEN

AFTER SEPTEMBER 11TH, 2001. Airport security took on a life of its own. The world, as a whole, accepted the violence of terrorism on a higher level, creating armed guards and intense screening procedures that had never been in place before. No matter how large or small the country, the need for this security had become apparent with the falling of the Twin Towers, despite the fact that in Europe, it had been already set in place years before due to terrorist bombings and political battles.

El Dorado International Airport in Bogotá, Colombia, was no different. While all the action was set forth in the airport of passengers passing through customs and working their way through various security details, the buzz of monitors ringing off for passengers who forgot to take off their belts or left a cellphone in their pocket was a frequent occurrence. The crew of men that armed and inspected each passenger as they moved through, were diligent in their duties despite the repetition and boredom of the job.

Those frontline workers were the main defense against

any potential illegal activity that entered into the people and nation of Colombia. Behind the back wall of customs inspection sat a large open room manned with various monitors and consoles, where men in their thirties and forties watched the monitors and focused in on people of interest they had pulled up from the flight manifest. Cups of coffee and crushed-out cigarette butts that had not made their way to the ashtray were the rule of the day. Much like their counterparts in the air traffic control, these men spent their days watching monitors and playing a high stakes game of life and death should they get things wrong.

"Ramone, I think you should come over here and see this," said the older man with graying temples and a cigarette dangling out of the corner of his mouth. His words were muffled from not being able to form all the letters, due to his mouth holding the cigarette, and his eyes barely braking contact with the screen he was watching.

"What's the problem here, Sanchez?" asked Ramone, the man that had no set spot in the office, instead, he roamed back and forth behind the men, peering into their monitors on occasion. His place of importance and as the boss was clear and defined. He watched over his troops, made sure they were doing the right thing, and if they called anything into question, it was his decision on what was done next.

"I got this guy here. It says on the manifest that his name is Falau, Michael Falau," said Sanchez.

"Has he done anything that seems off?" asked Ramone, folding his arms and peering over the shoulder of the man who had called him over in the first place.

"No, but he almost seems too comfortable," said the younger man. "I've got no past record of him being in the country and he hasn't done that much international travel. He just seems a little too calm for a guy who hasn't passed through any check points like we have here," said Ramone, referring to the fact that there were armed men carrying automatic rifles that were posted throughout the customs area.

"I don't know about this guy, he seems a little too scruffy to be anybody of importance," said Ramone, taking a long drag from the cigarette that had now come into his fingers and was quickly lit. "These are the guys that are the real ball-busters. They're the ones that we really don't know what's going on with them."

"I know what you mean. I can't put my finger on this guy. I don't know exactly what's wrong with him, but there's something wrong with him," said Sanchez tapping his finger on the screen as if he could get Falau to react through it. "I wonder if it's drugs."

"Could be, he might be muling things back to the US or any other country, but still, those guys try to fit in. I wonder what his game is. Is he really coming here by himself on some kind of pleasure trip?"

Pulling open the flight's manifest on another screen, Sanchez's hands started to type out the information from Falau that he had previously pulled from the manifest. Running his finger down the side of the screen of crunched up words as if they were trying to save space, Sanchez found his information on the man and clicked it, opening a file to him.

"I hope you don't mind, I'm gonna start a fresh file on this guy. Nothing to merge him with anything else," said Sanchez. "I just wonder when he comes back through, is he gonna have anything in the lining of that case or inside his stomach."

You really think this guy's a mule, don't you?" said Ramone patting the other man on the shoulder. "I think you got a good eye, kiddo."

"Kiddo? I've only been here five years less than you," said Sanchez laughing. "But I guarantee you, if we can grab this guy on his way back in, we've got him nailed."

"I'll bet a steak dinner on that," said Ramone. "We'll lock him in with the facial recognition as well. That way he can't pull any slick stuff and try to get around us on the way back."

Watching the monitor closely, the two men picked up on the shifting eyes of Falau and his assessment of the area. His moves were deliberate and smooth, not causing any attention to be had from lookers-on within the customs area. But for Ramone and Sanchez, having the ability to stop the tape, rewind, and watch again, they saw the subtlety of the man taking in everything around him.

"Could be CIA or FBI," said Ramone, who had now crossed his arms and was tapping his finger against the outer part of his biceps. "It would be a good cover for this guy. What does it say he's here for?"

"Business trip of some kind, not pleasure, just for a couple of days," said Sanchez, leaning back in his chair. "I don't know about you, boss, but I got a bad feeling about this guy. Not a terrorist, but I think definitely a drug runner. He just looks like a guy who's trying to fit in too much."

"I see what you mean. He's downplaying how he looks and how he presents himself. He's getting flustered at all the right movements and he's showing himself to be annoyed at certain times. Playing the stereotypical passenger in every way."

"Sure he's doing all that, but he's not doing enough to

draw people to him, and if he was really this annoyed with the pre-planned eye rolls, I think we would have seen this guy raise his voice by now," said Sanchez. "Or maybe he's just getting scared and he's a regular guy. Maybe he really is here on business. It's tough to make this guy out, but he's just way out of place right now."

"Might be because he looks like he's about six-foot five, and got the looks of a movie star, and he's hobbling through our Columbian airport with absolutely nobody with him."

"Not something we see every day, and it's not like we're a tourist destination or anything. We're workaday folks. I don't see what this guy would be doing here if it wasn't to get tied into the drug trade."

"Well, you know how it goes with these guys. They see the temptation of the money, and then that changes their life, but this guy is not gonna get away with it."

"It's funny what money can do to people. It always makes them do things they don't want to," said Sanchez leaning back in the chair.

"You did a good job with this one, Sanchez. Good eyes on tagging this guy. I'll make a point of making sure everyone knows it was you that did the job," said Ramone to the nodding head of Sanchez and the smile drawing across his face. "But I think we've done just about all we can do here. Now we gotta kick it upstairs."

Moving his way across the room, the older man kept his hands folded as his fingers still tapped away on his bicep, helping him think of exactly what his instincts were telling him about this passenger. Picking up the phone, he quickly dialed the number to his superior.

"Hello Sir, it's Ramone," said the man standing straighter up at attention as if his boss had been standing directly in front of him. "We have gentleman down here that we've flagged and think we might need to be on the look out for when he comes back. Could be drugs, could be something else. We're not really sure. He's just presenting himself as out of place and he's atypical of most of our passengers," said the man, as he then held himself in silence, listening to the reply.

"Yes, Sir, he's a white guy, came from the US. He's on the new flight that just came in out of Boston," said Ramone. "No, Sir, I'm not making this an issue of his race or that he's from the US, he's just... Well, I don't know how to put it. There's nothing really off about the guy, something just isn't quite right. He's just sparking everybody's interest down here on why he's in our country and what he's looking to do while he's here."

Holding still, the older man listened to a response on the other end of the phone. There was just a mumble to other people in the room. The voice on the other end wasn't raised or causing a commotion, but instead seemed to be authoritative and clear, causing no reaction from Ramone and the work that he had done.

"Thank you, Sir. We'll keep doing our job as diligently as possible. Let's hope that this guy has nothing wrong with his visit to us and that he goes back home with nothing more than what he came with."

ELEVEN

FEEDING the passkey into the slot in the door, the light turned green and he pushed the door open to his room at the Bogotá Hilton. Like so many of the other big hotel chains, the room was plain and simple. A large queen-size bed sat in the middle of the room. The desk and chair were along the far wall. Beside the large double sized window sat a small table and more comfortable-looking chairs.

Placing his bags on the table he examined the room, doubting they had time to get inside and add surveillance. He knew he couldn't fully examine things or he would blow his cover if they were watching from inside the room. *Better to keep playing the part given to him by Tyler*, he thought.

Falau walked to the bathroom to splash water on his face. Wiping himself off with the towel, he stared at himself beneath the strong lights of the mirror. It had been a long time since he had seen himself in this kind of light. He had aged, and it had snuck up on him. He had deep lines running down his face like men twice his age. He looked unkempt, despite the suit. He was miles away from the man he wanted to be.

"You killed me. It was your fault," said the woman in the back of his mind without warning.

Attempting to fend off the flashbacks, he ran the cold water and rubbed it on his face and in his hair, hoping the shock of the cold would do the trick. He pushed his hair back with the flat of his hand and walked quickly to the main room.

He opened the mini bar like a man on a mission and grabbed two nips from it. Not even waiting to see what they were, he poured them into a glass that sat on the table and took a long sip of the concoction. It went down hard and stung his throat, but it would do the job.

Sitting down in one of the more comfortable chairs he pulled another over to place his feet on. Staring out the window he took another drink while enjoying the skyline. In the distance several tall buildings stood out. One building had a light flashing from one window, but there was no way that the swift on-off, on-off was just someone turning a room light on and off, or some kids playing. This light was focused and directed. Studying it, there didn't seem to be any pattern to it. It simply flashed for short and long periods of time, but nothing over five seconds.

Hitting to the bottom of his drink Falau wondered who was flashing the light and for what purpose. *Could it be Vick?* he thought.

Like a lightning bolt from the blue he finally realized what the light was doing. It was Morse code. He recognized it from his short time in the military. Falau smiled and grabbed the paper and pencil from the desk. *It could be just some kids having fun*, he thought, but better to know what he was dealing with.

Copying down the dots and dashes of light he kept going until the sequence had repeated itself twice. Opening his smart phone, he deciphered the message and knew from the few simple words it said that it was from Vick.

"Corner of Carrera 9 and Calle 73. Tyler."

Tyler's name was all Falau needed to grab his coat and rush out the door.

TWELVE

THE ASH on the cigarette had grown long as it sat on its perch in the groove of the ashtray. The owner had somehow forgotten about it despite the constant stream of smoke drifting up from his desk.

Behind the desk sat a young man in his twenties. His olive skin and dark hair were not enough to charm ladies, so he focused his attention on his studies and work. That kind of dedication led him directly to the National Police of Colombia, straight out of university. And within a few short years the whiz kid had risen to the rank of lieutenant in the Special Operations Commandos. The SOC was tasked with being sent into action in situations considered high-risk tasks. But now he was stuck. The only way to move up the ladder was to have someone die above him, or to create a giant splash to draw positive attention onto himself. Regardless, neither of those seemed particularly possible as he sat in a one-window office at the city airport.

Carlos Rivera flipped through the hundreds of

photographs that lined his desk, all taken by the facial recognition software at the security area for incoming international travelers. Rivera felt like he had been tasked to find a needle in a haystack. Thousands of people each day entered the country through the airport, some were tagged in customs as being suspicious and it was his job to pick out the persons that did not belong. When he volunteered to work on the drug task force, he never thought it would involve sitting behind a desk at the airport. He was assured he had a very important role and if he screwed up on the task, he knew it would be his job.

Going through the photos for the third time, he was again taken aback by the American with a hardened face who had been detained but cleared to go on. The leadership felt he posed no threat and was ill-equipped to provide any kind of smuggling operation for the locals in that line of business. But Rivera remained uneasy with the man named Falau.

Turning to the computer where he had accessed the video, he scrolled to the moment when Falau was in the security area. Studying the man, he seemed oddly out of place. He was glancing to the side when he felt he was not being watched, a sign of a man who knew what he was doing. He didn't overplay his hand, but rather took sneaky looks to gauge the room, rather than someone looking to see if they were being surrounded. That is what normal passengers would do in that situation. Rivera remembered the words of his old trainer from years ago, *when people get detained they get claustrophobic. They feel like they're being held in. Watch out for the fight or flight response.* This man Falau showed none of that.

Flicking through the papers, the National Policeman found Falau's itinerary and scanned it. In no location did it show a clear meeting with any of the local coffee growers. Rivera knew that if this man was here for anything to do with farming, that his contacts would surely be within the drug trade.

This was exactly the kind of bust he had been waiting for —the one that slipped by the others—and he would pounce on it. All his life Rivera had wanted to exact revenge on the local drug cartel and its leader, The Butcher.

Rivera straightened himself up in his chair, remembering back to his childhood and the moment he learned how The Butcher had killed his brothers, who'd been dealing drugs in the streets. They refused to give up their money to The Butcher, so he responded by hanging them alive in the town square. He jammed a spike into their lower backs, up under their skin, and out through their necks. The brothers lived for several agonizing hours, but the community was too afraid to get involved for fear The Butcher would go after them. The ends of the poles were dug into the ground to put them on display for all to see. It was such a horrific sight that Carlos's parents would not let him see, but he had heard the stories around the neighborhood in all the graphic detail, painting an image he could never wipe from his mind.

Carlos knew that arresting Falau would disrupt The Butcher's operation and he'd get a minimal amount of revenge for the loss of his brothers. But any revenge would hold some satisfaction until the day that he could slip the cuffs on The Butcher himself and put him away for life.

Looking back to the itinerary, the name Hilton stood out. Carlos smiled. Hope you have a nice sleep, Mr. Falau, because I am going to be with you for the rest of your trip, he thought tapping on the picture.

Rivera stood up from his desk and grabbed his keys.

Moving to the door, he put his leather jacket on and took his motorcycle helmet from a hook on the door. Closing the door behind him Rivera knew this could be his one shot to advance himself in the eyes of the leaders of the National Police of Colombia.

THIRTEEN

WALKING through the front door of the hotel and onto the street, a gust of wind hit Falau, making sixty-five-degrees feel more like fifty-degrees. The busy street was alive with cars and pedestrians moving in every direction. Most pedestrians wore thick coats with their collars up to keep the wind at bay. Falau looked over the crowd, knowing this was making his job more difficult... high collars concealed faces and were good for covering people's eyes. The street looked like a mass of black jackets with only the tops of heads sticking out of them.

He moved down the steps and onto the sidewalk. Pushing his hands into his pockets, he hunched up his shoulders and started to walk at a casual pace. Being followed would be the worst thing that could happen now. He attempted to dance a fine line between walking too fast and trying not to appear too slow. Spotting a tail would be much harder on foot with so many people around. He knew any number of people could be going where he was, just by chance.

Staring into a store window, he used it to check the

reflection across the street. Everyone seemed to keep moving. Nobody even looked over. Opening his phone, he held it to his ear and began to speak.

"I know you want me to get the coat, but I have no idea what more you want," Falau snapped into the phone to nobody. Continuing to argue, he turned side-to-side constantly while talking and taking video with the phone.

"You want it so bad, just get the damn coat yourself... anything I get will just be a waste of time."

Turning the phone off, Falau was sure he had captured, on video, all the people that had been around him and in the area. Pushing the shop door open he went inside and headed straight for the women's coats.

"Can I help you, Sir?" asked an effeminate clerk as he strolled over to Falau. "I can see you have good taste. Are you shopping for your wife?"

"Actually, I am getting some pictures of different styles, then she can get an idea of them and we can come back and pick it out. You know, saves me from having to be here if she tries on thirty different styles."

The clerk smiled and nodded at Falau with a good amount of condescension towards the fashion impaired American. "Well, if she likes one, please send her to us and we will take good care of her."

"Thanks," said Falau as the clerk strolled away.

Taking out his phone Falau turned down the volume and started to watch the video while pulling out different coats and acting like he was taking photographs. The faces all seemed normal. If he was being followed, the guy was very good and was not tipping his hand. *Am I just paranoid?* Falau thought to himself. *Who the hell even knows I'm here?*

Getting back out onto the street he kept his pace steady

and even, stopping at the occasional shop to look inside the window, keeping up his façade. Passing the Universidad Santo Tomás he got to the intersection of Carrera 9 and Calle 73. There was a beehive of activity, taxis going up to the sidewalks and people hopping in. People cutting across the street against the lights. The screech of brakes from a driver who had not been watching where he was going. It was organized chaos at its finest. A kind of ballet, where all the dancers were moving on their own to different styles of music. It was just a matter of time until two crashed into one another.

A car screeched to a halt in front of Falau. A taxi sign adorned the top of the car and it was clear this was a bootleg taxi, as nothing indicated it was part of one of the big companies working the streets. Falau knew these guys always worked harder to get their fares and had to stay one step ahead of the law. Normally they were also a bit riskier than the normal taxi because they were operating on the wrong side of the law. The driver leaned over, pulling down the window. "Need a lift?"

Staring into the car, Falau saw a woman driving. She was attractive, with dark hair and blue eyes. Despite seeing none of her skin, other than her face, Falau could see she was strong and fit, and seemed to be the kind of woman that could handle herself in a fight with a man.

"You need a ride or what, Mister? Tyler said you might need a ride."

Hearing Tyler's name was all Falau needed to take this ride from a stranger. If she were working for someone after him then they had done their homework. Falau reached down to open the door, with a loud creak, and hopped into the back seat. No sooner had Falau hit the seat than the woman screeched away from the curb and burst into the middle of the intersection. Heading next to a side street, the tires squealed on the turn.

"Did Tyler teach you how to drive?" snapped Falau, but it was met with silence from the woman. Again and again Falau attempted to engage the woman with some kind of conversation, but was constantly met with no response.

"Can you speak?" Falau asked her with sarcasm and building frustration.

"Yeah. Shut up," said the woman, letting Falau know exactly where he stood with her.

Cutting the wheel hard again she pulled into a taxi parking garage. Keeping her speed up she raced to the far end of the garage and pulled into the spot next to several other cars that looked exactly like the one she was driving.

"Out! Now! Follow me and shut up!" demanded the woman, not waiting for Falau to answer. The door swung open and she started to walk away, causing Falau to scramble to catch up to her.

The sudden sound of more tires screeching made Falau look back. The car was being driven away by a woman with dark hair and a man in the backseat. She had thought of everything to keep the cover alive, just in case they were being watched. Falau was sure that by the time they had hit the garage entrance the man would have on clothing similar to his and nobody would know the difference. The woman continued to move at a swift pace as they exited out the back of the garage. Reaching down to grab Falau by the hand, she dropped back next to him giving the appearance that the two were a couple.

"This is all very sudden. I don't even know your name," said Falau sarcastically.

"Don't flatter yourself," said the woman, smiling and leading him to the door of the building next to the garage. She then unlocked the door to the apartment building and went inside. Rushing up one flight of steps she led them into the hall and to the first door on the right. Apartment 2J. Unlocking the door they went in. All Falau knew was this woman knew Tyler's name, and nothing more. He wondered if he'd just walked into an ambush, following nothing more than the name of a friend.

Falau closed the door behind him, and across the room the woman closed the curtain. Turning back to him, the two measured each other up.

"My name is Carla Romero, but my friends call me Vick."

"You're Vick?" questioned Falau, his forehead furrowing as he shook his head. "Sorry, I was expecting someone a little more... a man."

"I get that a lot. Guess the name does its job as a disguise. So, you're the guy they sent to get The Butcher. You must be some kind of a badass, right. Ex-CIA? FBI? Navy seal?"

"Nothing like that. I just needed a job."

"Just needed a job?" Carla raised her eyebrows. "Okay, I understand the need to keep things close to the vest. I respect that."

Falau smiled, walked over to the window and peeked out the curtain.

"So, Falau, my job is to give you all the info I have so you can take down The Butcher. You need to listen up, because this guy is not just a sick son of a bitch, but he is smart. Really smart. As a kid he could've gone to any university he liked, but he didn't see the sense in going to school where he knew more than the professors. He wanted to pull his family out of poverty, so he looked to drugs. He is so smart, he knows not to be the top man. The Police always want to get the top man. It is a better show for the cameras. He knows that it is a lot better to be down the line. You can keep low and still make millions of dollars. It has only been the last few years he turned into The Butcher. His brother stole a million dollars from him and put out a hit on him, looking to take over the operation. He felt he needed to send a message to everyone who might think he was weak. So, he paid the zookeepers not to feed the lions for two weeks. He then dragged his brother into the zoo with the help of a few men. Then they threw him to the lions in the middle of the day. Families were there. Schoolchildren were there. Story has it, they even put blood in his hair to get the lions to attack. He is not a nice guy at all."

"Well I wasn't thinking of taking him out for coffee. I just want to get him and bring him back," said Falau. "Where is he?"

The woman sat on the sofa, grabbed the top of the coffee table and opened it like a car hood, exposing several handguns hidden inside. "I prefer the 9 mm, but most guys like to brag about having the big one, so here's a .45 for you."

Falau smirked at Carla's ribbing. The more he spoke with her the more he liked her. She gave as good as she got. She was a fighter, but still maintained her feminine side through it all. There was nothing overly masculine about her, but her ability to take care of any situation in front of her was undeniable, even without having seen it.

"As I'm sure you know he runs drugs up to Miami and other spots on the east coast of North America and some places in Europe. Miami is the easiest because he could always fall back into Cuba if things got messy with the Coast Guard. He does it all through a warehouse over at the import/export station here in the city. He has everyone paid off so it is easy to hide drugs. He has at least thirty men working for him at the warehouse and on the street. The most notice you will ever have before they know he's gone is about two hours. If they can't find him for that long they will be looking for him."

"Thanks for the info. What is the address of the warehouse?" asked Falau

"I will show you."

"Sorry, but I work alone. This is my mission," interrupted Falau.

"Mr. Falau, I'm coming with you. I want this guy nailed just like you, and I'm going to help. Besides there's no way in the world you're getting into that warehouse without me. They will see you coming a mile away," she replied, smiling the smile of a person who knows they are right.

Falau looked to the ground, shook his head and wiped his face with his hand. "Okay, but I'm the lead. You fall in with my orders and no other way around it. You got it?"

"Sir. Yes Sir," quipped the woman Falau could not help but like.

FOURTEEN

COCAINE WAS KING. And it had been for a very long time. The fields across Colombia, they were hidden away from the police, and their supply for the drug trade held poppy and marijuana as far as the eye could see. The marijuana yielded a profit, but nothing in comparison to that of the cocaine trade. It was how Colombia had made its mark, with drug trade across the world. A vast, intricate system of men shuttling cocaine out of the country, moving it up the coasts, and finally having it land in the United States, or the country of their choosing, all done through individuals, in a closed lip tight society. The ultimate goal, was to have it hit the streets and have the customers love it. Then prices could go up and the supply could tighten.

But after the year 2000, things had changed, heroin had opened the door, and prices had dropped severely. Heroin was smaller to transport, easy to use, and was able to be hidden in just about anything, provided that the source of the drugs didn't get too greedy and try to move too much at one time. It had been a changing of the times, a shift in production, and now, less than 20 years after heroin had made a bigger splash than it ever had before, pharmaceuticals were coming into play. None more so than fentanyl and carfentanil. Fentanyl was considered a miracle drug by many, easing the pain of suffering from cancer patients and people with chronic pain. The trouble was, the addiction was quick and merciless. It dug in to whoever took it, grabbing a hold of them and not letting go. The easing of the pain was simply compiled and then the person was hooked without a chance of return.

Sitting back in an office at the top of a set of wooden stairs in a distribution center in Colombia, The Bucher sat with his feet up on a desk and twirling a pencil between his fingers, like a drummer does with the drumstick.

The man's face was jagged and edgy. It was weathered hard and leathered from the time he had spent outdoors, being homeless and struggling for most of his life. The cartels in the drug trade pulled the man up from nothing, giving him a life of what any would consider extravagance. Unwilling to let it go, The Bucher doubled down on his work, pushing himself harder and the people around him.

"Did you get the shipment?" said The Bucher, snapping his voice and waving his finger at the man that sat across the room

"We're making the boost this afternoon, looks like a good amount too. I think it's gonna turn over really well on the street," said the younger man, typing on his keyboard and maintaining communication with the people that were necessary for the business to run smoothly.

"So when are they gonna get it here?" asked The Bucher, tossing the pencil onto the desk next to his legs where his feet were comfortably raised up. "This is fucking pointless.

We should have just gone and got it ourselves, instead of having these little ragtag gangs go get it for us."

"Boss, you were the one who said you wanted us to be removed from it, so we get these guys to do the job and then we don't have to even be there if they get popped," said the younger man.

"I didn't count on them being such morons and not knowing what the hell they were doing," said The Bucher, now sliding a knife out of a sheath that sat on his hip. Spinning the knife in his hand, the blade pushed against one of his finger nails on the other hand boring a small hole into the nail as it spun. "This is why, if you want it done right, you gotta do it yourself. These guys, if they get popped, they'll try to roll over, and talk about us. They think we're gonna bail them out, wait and see, then they're gonna try to turn us in to try and save their own asses."

"But you have half the police department on the payroll, they're not gonna get anywhere with it. Even if it did end up in court you'd have that crushed before anything could happen," said the younger man, shifting in this chair and looking over to The Bucher. The man watched The Bucher hold himself in concentration, still continuing to spin the knife with the tips of his fingers into the nail of his other finger. He admired The Bucher for his strength, perseverance, and ability to pull himself out of the worst situations that most couldn't endure. The childhood of dirt floors, before having his mother and father taken from him by the cartels for refusal to move their product into the United States, his siblings dispersed and moved all over the country with willing family that would take them in. But his fate was not the same. He went to a family friend, only to endure two years of physical and sexual abuse at the hands of an alcoholic man and a wife that turned a blind eye to the abuse to the young boy. By the time he was ready to leave, The Bucher had committed his first murder before he had even seen his teenage years. The man that had taken him in for two years was found mysteriously dead with his neck slit and his genitals removed in a back alley in the city of Bogotá. Due to the man being nothing more than a work-a-day common man, who struggled to make ends meet, no fuss was kicked up over his loss and things moved on despite its gruesome nature. It was easier to blame the gangs and drug runners for the death rather than look at the little boy who lived in his home.

"We need that carfentanil, that's a game changer for us, it's a game changer for everybody," said The Bucher. "The stuff is far more powerful than fentanyl. We can break it down, give it out in smaller doses, turn over a higher profit much faster and the people that get that crap are pharmacists. None of those guys carry guns."

"Are we sure that this is the kinda thing that we wanna get into, Sir? It seems like we're taking an awful big chance on having people boost the product in transit."

Letting his eyes drift up from his knife, The Bucher grabbed the handle of the knife and tightened it in his hand. Sliding his feet to the floor, he propped himself up straight in his chair looking across at the young man.

"Well, we can't exactly grow carfentanil. It comes from a different place, but we do have the ability to make the heroin. And carfentanil goes hand-in-hand with heroin. We get that carfentanil out on the streets, people start taking it, they love it, and when it runs out or it's a limited supply, they're gonna turn back to the heroin. We get the hook in them a lot faster and a lot deeper," said The Bucher looking at the young man, "Did you not understand that concept before?"

"Oh, I understand what the plan is. I was just wondering if it was too much risk we were taking for the reward we're gonna get on the other end," said the young man putting his eyes back on the screen, and feeling the pressure from the gaze of The Bucher. "I was just trying to help out and give a different perspective."

Pushing up out of his seat, The Bucher stood up, holding his knife down by his side and walking slowly across the room. "So you thought you'd just give me a little advice?" said The Bucher moving his way over and stationing himself up close to the side of the man whose eyes were locked on his computer screen. "You thought you'd just talk out of turn, and tell *me*, the way things go. You were going to let me know, that in all your vast years of experience, that you think this is the most profitable way to do things. You think your way of pushing just straight heroin on the street is gonna yield a million dollars a day?"

"I am... I'm sorry Sir. I... I didn't mean it. I was just trying to let you know what I was thinking. I'm sorry if I spoke out of turn," said the young man hoping his apology would satisfy his boss but not daring to make eye contact with him.

"You've never killed a man, have you?" asked The Bucher.

"No Sir. That's not my area of expertise."

"That's right. You're a computer man. We brought you in because you know how to hack systems, you know how to get us into the police, you know how to get us into national security, you know how to get us into each and every pharmacy and hospital, so we know exactly what they have for medications on hand," said The Bucher sticking the tip of the knife into the desk where the man was working. "Did anybody ever talk to you about helping with strategy, or financial planning for our business and its future?"

Feeling a slight bit of relief and that his expertise was being noticed by The Bucher, the young man turned slightly in his chair and quickly looked up to his boss. "No Sir, but I'm happy to help in any way that I can."

In a clean, fluid motion, The Bucher grabbed the man by the back of the hair, pulling his head back and pushing his own face within inches of the other man's face. "Maybe you should realize your place in this organization. The biggest part of our organization is following the rules, and you are deciding to step outside your area of expertise and give advice on another area. I don't want to hear it!" said The Bucher. "Men have died for far less than what you're doing right now. So you should check yourself, and focus yourself on your job at hand, or I could simply just cut off your hands and leave you to pick rags in the street, and put on shows for change down at the local square."

"I'm sorry, Sir. I... I... I didn't mean it. I'll... I'll stay with what I know, Sir. I won't speak unless spoken to," said the stammering man whose mind began to pray to God for a leniency from The Bucher.

"I can't have this kind of thing, I can't have men like you deciding to do different things on their own," said The Bucher reaching back with his free hand and taking the knife that had stuck into the desk. Drawing the knife forward slowly, the light caught a glint off the edge and reflected in the man's eyes. Despite his head being pulled back, his eyes looked down as hard as they could and saw the knife moving slowly toward him, before nestling itself along the left side of his neck, directly pressed against his carotid artery.

"From right here it just takes a slice. That's all it would take. Just open up that artery that runs along your neck, that carries all of that blood up to your brain. You'd simply bleed out. Drip by drip, just like a car losing oil. But once it stopped flowing that blood up to your brain, you'd only last a very short time. You'd fall to the floor, you'd have some consciousness, but by that point, your heart would be pumping the blood out of your neck in a spraying fashion with each pump. Every drip would get all over the place. It would be a whole mess for me to have cleaned up, and right now, it's about the only thing that's saving you."

Afraid to mumble even the slightest syllable, the young man held still, making sure not to do anything that might cause The Bucher to react and use his knife.

"It's a shame. I had high hopes for you. And I actually liked talking to you," said The Bucher. "But I can't have this; I can't have it at all. So I'm gonna give you a choice, young man, and it's a simple choice at that," said The Bucher, pressing the knife harder against the man's neck. "I can kill you. I can end your life right now. I would simply cut your throat and I would make it fast and easy. You'd die within moments. I'd plunge this blade straight into your heart, and then rip it as hard as I could to the side, trying to slice the heart that gives you life into two. Or you can take the punishment. And I think the punishment for a man who's behaved such as you would be to make sure you don't talk again. To make sure you knew as a constant reminder that your life is my life. And I can choose to do what I want with your life."

The Bucher let the room come to quiet. Silence fell over only to be broken by the work being done in the warehouse down below. A gunshot or a scream wouldn't raise an eyebrow to anybody working on the warehouse floor. The sounds had all been heard before, and now had become commonplace.

"So I'm gonna give you a choice my friend. A choice that I don't often give to many people. You should feel proud," said The Bucher. "This is what you get to pick between. As I said I could kill you and end it all right now, or I can blind you taking your sight from both eyes. I could make you deaf, plunging a sharp heated metallic rod into your ear, destroying your eardrums and letting you never hear a word again. Or I could take one of your feet, chop it off, bring it to a stump and have you forever spend the rest of your life either in a wheelchair or using crutches. But I leave that decision to you. And with God as my witness, by the end of work today, one of those options will be fulfilled."

Letting go of the young man's hair, The Bucher let the knife slowly drag along the neck of the young man, creating a slight cut in the skin that drew up small beads of blood. Pulling himself up from the desk, The Bucher placed the knife into the sheathing again, moving back to his desk and placing his feet back upon it.

"I expect your decision in the next five minutes."

FIFTEEN

AS DAY TURNED TO NIGHT, Falau and Carla drove down a side street and pulled to the side of the road under trees that hung over the car. A street light flickered on and off about ten-feet behind them and most of the light from the main roads was muted on the quiet street.

Cracking the driver side window, a sudden cool breeze caused Falau to tighten up his coat as they sat side by side watching the end of the street.

The moment wasn't lost on the man who had lost his love so many years ago. This was the first time he sat in a vehicle with a woman since the accident. The parallels were undeniable. A strong woman with a sense of humor. An instant attraction that was more than just physical. She stirred something in Falau that he felt had been laid to rest a long time ago and was not wanting to relive again.

The activity in the warehouse was constant. People coming and going in all areas. Several forklifts moving pallets of merchandise to various locations. There was a large chain-link fence around the property and there was only one gate in and out. The security was lackluster defined by young men who glossed over at the constant coming and going of people, trucks, and equipment. The same thing day in and day out created a malaise on the young men whose minds were on more exciting times when they were off work.

"Tyler gave me something he said you would like," Carla said, reaching into the inside pocket of her jacket. "If these things really work it will be true what they say about him."

"What? That he is a genius?"asked Falau.

Carla turned her head to Falau with a look of total confusion on her face. "You know about that?"

"Tyler and I go way back. I know what he's capable of," said Falau, not looking away from the warehouse. "Tyler is that mix between genius and insane that few people can walk. He's the Tesla of black ops."

Carla produced a square piece of what look like cellophane and pulled it into two pieces. Leaning toward the windshield, she pressed one piece in front of herself and one piece in front of Falau.

"Look straight into it," she said, gazing into the new addition to the window.

"Oh, I'll be damned. Binoculars made from cellophane!" exclaimed Falau trying to make sense of how Tyler could create something like that.

"This defies everything I know about magnification and how it works," said a stunned Carla.

"I told you the guy's Tesla," said Falau shaking his head in amazement. "Unbelievable."

The two partners resumed watching the goings on with different workers at the warehouse and what tracks they were taking as they went to and from the building. Looking for a pattern in the chaos of what they did was a tall task.

"That's him," said a cold and detached Carla. "The one inside the guard shack at the entrance to the warehouse."

Adjusting his eyes, Falau drew his attention to the man he felt looked different to the picture he'd seen of him. He looked harder and more aggressive. A deep scar ran down his right cheek. Jagged and deep, it was clear it had not been treated properly in a hospital. It may not have ever been stitched up. His goatee was unkempt and hanging low, six-inches at least from his chin. A cigarette dangled from his mouth, glowing bright orange every few moments when he took a drag from it. He was the alpha male of the group, there was no doubt about that. Falau watched as the others changed their course so as to not converge with him or get into his line of sight. Word was spreading fast with the outside workers that The Butcher was at the door. The Butcher's arms moved up and down with pointing in various directions as he attempted to get his directions across to the workers in the area. It was clear that The Butcher did not keep to his section of the warehouse but had a hand in everything that went on, including boosting items from other importers and exporters when he thought he could make a quick buck on the street with the stolen merchandise.

Without looking away, Falau tapped on the steering wheel. "Looks like a tough guy. He could be problematic down the road. When should we hit him?"

"This place has no slow time. Anytime is good as any other. We just have to get him alone," replied Carla.

Turning his head, he saw her sitting with her back against the passenger side door, and without warning his mind flashed, causing him to gasp for breath.

The beautiful woman from the flashback was now mixed with Carla. Falau's mind drifted between them, overlapping them, and blood started dripping down from Carla's hairline and covering her face. Shards of glass sprung up in her cheeks and her forehead. The light left her eyes and her mouth dropped open. "You killed me," she said, "It was your fault. The light was red. You know the light was red. You killed me." The words came out of Carla's mouth but it was not her voice. It was the voice of the other woman.

Falau's mind suddenly jerked back to the present. Sweat ran off his face. His hand gripped the steering wheel hard and he had an overwhelming urge to run away. Tightening his body he tried to push the thoughts from his mind with shear force and will.

"No. No. No!" snapped Falau at the images in his head, overrun by the evil that had taken up residence in his mind. A hand grabbed his and pulled it away from the keys before he turned the engine over.

"What are you doing?" asked Carla.

"I didn't kill you!! It isn't my fault!" barked the terrified man as his eyes darted around the car trying to make sense of things.

"Falau! You okay? Falau!" Placing her hand on his face she pulled his eyes toward her. They were out of focus and looked right through the young woman. "Falau!"

"Yeah! What? I'm good now!" yammered Falau as he dropped back into the present, unable and unwilling to explain what was happening to him. "Sorry, I was just thinking about the car accident a long time ago."

"I understand. Some things never go away. You can live them over and over again like they're happening for the first time right in front of you," sympathized Carla, and Falau immediately sensed a kinship with the woman he had only met a short time ago. He could tell from her voice that she understood about the flashbacks and how anyone could fall into them without warning.

"I call it my dark half. It pops up occasionally. I manage it the best I can."

"Your dark half? I like that. I have one of those too. I remember my brothers being killed. Every sound, every look from other people, every smell in the air. They were slaughtered like dogs for no good reason. Each was given a Colombian necktie. Do you know what that is?" asked Carla, her eyes drifting away from Falau. He could feel her pain with each word, knowing she too was seeing everything she said in her mind's eye.

"No"

"You see, if they think you're a snitch or you're really pissing people off they give you a Colombian necktie. They cut your throat so deep that it cuts into your windpipe. Then they reach up and pull your tongue out through the hole. Sends a message to everyone what they will do to you if you cross them. But for a kid to see your brothers like that causes something to be taken from your soul. Something that you can never get back. I walked out of the door to go to school, and found my two brothers with the Colombian neckties impaled on the rod-iron fence at the front of the house. You stop being a kid right then and there. I didn't scream and I didn't cry. I just got angry."

Looking out into the distance, Falau searched for the right words to say. It was clear her pain was equal in every way to his. She just managed to use it as fuel to go after the killer. She wanted revenge for what The Butcher did. Falau felt a stream of shame run over him for not having the resolve that Carla showed. He had fallen into a shell and hid from the world after his trauma. He'd gained nothing, and had not grown at all from it. He simply gave up on life and was willing and waiting to die.

"My brothers were good guys. There was no way they were into anything like drug running. They had a future without any of that."

"Did Carlos kill them?" inquired Falau.

"No. But he gave the order. Nobody kills anyone in the city without him giving the order first."

"I'm sorry you had to deal with that. It's not fair."

"Thank you. That's why this one is so important to me. I need to take this guy down hard. I thought we had him in the trial but he has too much money and too much power over the government. Now we get revenge and justice my way."

"I'm happy to help you in any way I can. I think it's time we take a walk and get a closer look at things, and see if we can find a way to pay The Butcher a little visit," said Falau with a hard look on his face.

"Let's go," responded the woman who had only justice on her mind.

SIXTEEN

THE LEATHER CLAD man backed into the shelter of the tree. Rivera sat on a stone wall in the shadows just 10-feet from his Yamaha YZF R6 motorcycle, a bike built for speed and precision. People passed by barely glancing at the man smoking a cigarette and dressed in leather riding gear.

Rivera thought about the couple that sat in the car two blocks away from him. Questions came to mind without answers. Who was the woman? Why were they watching the warehouse? What happened to the cab they were in?

The questions kept coming, but he knew he was lucky to even know where they were. If not for the closed-circuit TV cameras based around the city he would've never seen Falau leave the hotel to get picked up by the woman. She had to be part of the drug smuggling ring. It was the only thing that made any sense to Rivera. Rivera searched his mind as he watched the woman in the car reach across and take the man's face into her hand. *They must be using farming equipment to move the drugs. Maybe they load the equipment in the fields and then move the equipment back to the transport area? Then the guy, Falau, goes home saying no sale with equipment filled with drugs?*

The car door swung open, causing Rivera to drop his cigarette. He held back against the wall, trying not to reveal himself. The woman and the man got out and moved onto the sidewalk.

The couple started walking up the street about a couple of feet apart. Their demeanor made it clear they were just business partners.

Rivera hopped on his motorcycle and put on his helmet. Turning the key, the bike came to life. Getting involved without official permission from the Commandos of the National Police was something clearly he knew could backfire on him, but if he was ever going to push his name to the top of the list this just might be the case to do it. He was willing to take the chance to get the big payoff.

Rivera pushed the bike up to its normal speed until he was within twenty-feet of his targets. He revved the engine and popped the clutch, causing the bike to chirp its tires and lurch forward. Instinctively the couple looked as he raced past them.

There was no doubt it was Falau and the woman. Now the question was, what were they doing outside the warehouse if they were part of the smuggling operation?

Approaching the corner Rivera slowed down and took a right, and once out of eyesight of the couple he pumped his fist in excitement.

SEVENTEEN

A MOTORCYCLE SPED past them in a commotion of sound and speed.

"Stupid kid," Falau said, annoyed.

They continued walking up the street while attempting to pass as lovers. Falau reached down and took Carla's hand, and held it tight in his own. Still focusing her gaze up the street she questioned him. "What is this all about?"

"No man would walk the street with a woman that looks as good as you without making sure everyone knew she was taken. I'm just completing the disguise."

Carla laughed softly. "Really? How nice to know you think I'm attractive. I was beginning to think you were dead inside."

"It's obvious," Falau said, teasing, "just like it's obvious that I'm extremely attractive. No need to agree. Like I said, it's obvious."

Carla let out another laugh she knew was far too loud and would draw attention if anyone heard it. The couple was now less than a block away from the warehouse and its high chain link fence.

"To make this more believable, just in case anyone is watching, we may as well do this thing right."

Taking a step in front of Falau, she stopped him in his tracks. Pulling herself in close to him she looks deep into his eyes. "Put your hands on my hips," she whispered and Falau did as he was instructed.

Pulling herself up—and Falau down—she kissed him gently on the lips and then lowered herself into a hug, dropping her face against his chest.

Falau held his breath, absorbing all the affection he could. Despite knowing this was all part of a cover, he couldn't help but enjoy the feeling of her touch. It'd been years since anyone had touched him with such affection.

Carla pulled back and put her arms around Falau's waist, and he followed her lead doing the same. Without warning she slid her hand into the back pocket of his jeans, catching Falau off guard.

"This is what makes it really believable," she said while squeezing his buttocks.

Falau chuckled while looking down at what he now considered a new friend. Her humor and skill was all he needed to enjoy her.

The two got closer to the corner and rounded to the right. Continuing their giggling and the sounds of a couple in love, they walked unnoticed two-hundred-yards from the entrance to the facility. At this distance, the security lights got more intense and they were able to make out the staff clearly. Another hundred yards down the street and the property of the facility ended with a road that turned into the left amid more chain-link fence.

"No cameras," commented Falau. "I would have thought that an important building containing exports would be covered in heavy security."

"No need for cameras. This place is twenty-four hours a day, seven days a week, and three-hundred-and-sixty-five days a year. Cameras would just document all the illegal shit going on in there. They post this place as a government building so they can do what they want, whenever they want. Government sanctioned drug smuggling brought to you by Colombia," replied Carla, trying but failing to keep her temper in check.

They moved to the side street on the left and hugged close to the fence line, searching for a place was that covered by the high stacks of pallets.

"This is the spot," directed Carla, dropping to one knee where one of the support bars on the fence stood. Her hands worked quickly as she pulled away the section of wire that ran along the bottom of the fence. She had noticed that the wire had been broken at that point, most likely from a piece of equipment breaking it in two. "Pull it up for me!"

Falau again did as instructed and lifted the fence, and Carla rolled under it. Without hesitation, she stood pressing her back against the chain-link, holding it off the ground and waving Falau through. Falau dropped to the ground and rolled under the fence, and Carla put it back into position right behind him.

Behind the pallets, Falau wiped the dirt and earth from his pants and shirt.

"Falau?" called Carla in a stern whisper. "I have our targets," she said pointing to the closest side of the warehouse.

Gently, Falau moved to her position, attempting to make

as little noise as possible. From fifty-yards away he could see two men had exited from the loading door of the warehouse. The men were of average size and appeared to be sneaking off for a cigarette break.

"They are perfect," he whispered. "We just need to be stealthy."

Carla nodded in agreement and motioned for Falau to stay where he was. As she started to move forward she felt Falau grab her arm.

"Where are you going?"

"I can take care of this."

"Sure you can, but we're a team."

"Right," she replied sarcastically. "I need you to provide cover in case things go wrong. You know, with the gun."

Trying not to reveal his embarrassment, he nodded, and she was on her way. He felt as if he wanted to protect her, but was not sure why. She was more than capable by herself, and they had only just met.

Creeping ever so slowly, she moved to within twenty-yards. Keeping low to the ground, she looked through the pallets and could see the men still holding their position. One dropped his cigarette and his left leg twisted to put it out. Time was short. She needed to make the move.

Reaching into her shirt she found the strap of her bra. Rolling it to the side she pulled out a small four-inch-long tube that was not much more than a swizzle stick.

Patting the back of the tube, two small darts fell into her hand. Removing the dart caps, she loaded one into the tube. Staying low to the ground she took aim at the man on the right. She took a deep breath, making sure not to have the tube in her mouth as she did, having heard far too many stories of people sucking in their own poisonous darts. The quick thrust of breath, and the dart rushed through the air, going through the man's pants and causing him to smack his leg like he was stung by a bee.

Wasting no time another dart was loaded and fired off, causing the same reaction from the second man. As the drug entered the men's bodies it made its way into their blood stream instantly racing its way up to their brains.

Before the men could realize what was happening they were hit with a wave of nausea and then dropped to the ground, unconscious, from the rush of chemicals that entered their systems.

Falau moved forward when given the signal to move up, seeing the two men lying on the ground. "Dead?" he questioned, staring at the bodies.

"No, just gone to sleep for the next twelve hours and will wake up with a hell of a headache."

Not wasting time with more chit chat with Falau, Carla made her way over to the bodies, grabbed one by the shirt, and dragged it behind the pallets. Falau helped her, once he realized what she was doing.

"Take their badges," she demanded

"Got it."

With the bodies hidden under a stack of pallets, and new security credentials, the partners felt more comfortable walking in the open. The loading door was now shut and the only way into the building was the main entrance. Trying to conceal themselves, the couple kept close to the building so as not to look out of place. The closer they got to the entrance the more they allowed themselves to be seen. Now walking with purpose, the two were acting like they were in charge of the operation at the warehouse.

Stopping at the guard shack, at the entrance of the

warehouse, a young man sat inside listening to a baseball game in Spanish.

"ID?" he questioned, not looking away from the paperwork that sat on his desk.

Pulling the badge on the lanyard up, the man waved them through, barely glancing their way.

"Go ahead," he mumbled

Carla and Falau entered the operation with a smile. They both felt the same way. We are in!

EIGHTEEN

THE WAREHOUSE SPREAD OUT WIDE and high. Falau felt it looked more like an aircraft hangar than the inside of a warehouse. The ceiling approached forty-feet, making the main area easily able to house stacks of cars or boats. The facility was alive with activity that showed no indication of the time of day. They ran the same way twenty-four hours a day.

The floor stretched out far to the right and left, and in each direction there were rows of products waiting to be moved into the next location. At the front of the aisle was a sign indicating the company that owned that space. Most of the names were unrecognizable to the common person but in the world of importing and exporting all the big names were there. The others were a constant rotation of young up and comers thinking they could crack the nut that so many others had failed to do.

Seeing others wearing a badge the same as the ones they had on, Carla watched them question people about what was happening and then move on. The conversations were short and to the point. The questioners showed not comradery with the people they were questioning. They were clearly a grade ahead of the others and held a place of authority.

"We hit the jackpot," she said, walking with an air of confidence. "We have luck on our side."

"Why?" asked Falau.

"The badges were for inspectors. They think we are here to look at the merchandise going in and out," said Carla, letting a smile cross her face that was normally held in stone.

Falau nodded his head without changing his expression. He knew the inspector badge was a major advantage but also knew it would not ensure they get to The Butcher to secure him for transport. It was just an asset at this point and would only be as good as they could make it.

Spotting a worker who had stepped in and spoke with The Butcher at the front gate, Falau nudged Carla, showing her what he had seen but not saying a word.

The worker made his way over to the sign that said, 'Jetway International'. Soon he vanished out of sight down the opening that had products stacked twenty-feet high on each side.

"Exporters. Figures," remarked Carla. "Now... how do they do it? You have to hide the drugs, but in what?"

"Anything they can get their hands on," said Falau "I have heard stories that they will even break down the drugs and mix it with the rubber that lines the suit case. That way anyone can open it up and see there is nothing inside. It's not until the dogs get their noses working that they get caught. ""

"I don't think The Butcher is that smart," said Carla. "He doesn't care if his guys get caught. He will just steal another batch and try to move that."

The two started to walk over to the Jetway International

location, trying to exude a sense that they were in charge of what was happening. With their heads held high, they looked about as if they were examining everything. It was clear that a conversation with the examiners was not a good thing for the workers, and could only lead to trouble for any one of the companies operating on the warehouse.

"Jetway International is a legitimate company. They've been around since I was a kid. The company set up here in Colombia for the cheap labor, and then ship everything back to the States, Canada, and Europe. I wonder if the management is in on what's happening with the drug operation?"

Falau stopped and went over to a box whose label said it held children's toys. He popped the top off the box and pulled out a baby doll and looked it over. "My guess is that they know what they're doing. I'm sure The Butcher has intimidated them to the point that they let him do whatever he wants. They keep their mouths closed, or they and their families die."

Carla rolled her eyes, knowing Falau was right. The Butcher would not give up any amount of money when he could just kill—or threaten to kill—and get the same results. People had a way of doing what they are told when the man telling them what to do is known for the most brutal murders in the area.

As they strolled down the aisle, they saw a staggering range of products to be shipped by Jetway International. They moved everything from coffins to toys, from baby products to prosthetic limbs. Falau could envision the way in which any of the products could be used to move drugs, and with such a large quantity of merchandise being shipped they could parcel out the drugs in small amounts over a vast number of concealed items.

"Hey! What you are doing down here? This is personnel only!" barked an overweight Colombian no more than forty-years-old. The man could not have been more average in any way. His height, complexion, and even mustache did not stand out. He didn't break stride until he was within a foot of the couple.

"You two need to get out of here, right now. This is a personnel area only!" declared the man, pointing in the opposite direction and acting like his job was on the line if anyone found them where they were.

"Inspection," Falau said coldly, not making eye contact with the man but pointing to the badge that hung from his shirt. "We need to check you guys, just like every other company in the facility. Today we got stuck with you. Let's make the best of things."

"You guys must be new. We don't get inspected much. My bosses worked it out that everything gets inspected early so we can ship faster," replied the worker, trying to explain the arrangements without divulging too much information.

"That's not what we were told," Carla interjected.

"Hey lady!" said the worker. "I'm talking to the man."

Falau looked out the corner of his eye, to see the red rise up on Carla's cheeks. The worker had lit the fuse to a time bomb and he didn't even know it. Falau wanted to smile but instead he held his tongue and waited for the show to start.

"Excuse me? What did you say?" the feisty woman started with a hard edge to her words. "You listen to me. I can make your life a living hell. I can make your team unpack every single box, and you will have to lay out each item so I can inspect them all personally. I can hold off everything that you have a shipment for, and put it all in quarantine for thirty days. How would your boss like that? How'd you like it if I tell him you were not following procedure and decided to insult an inspector? My guess is he wouldn't be happy. I swear to you that if you do not start giving me the respect I deserve, that my team and I will climb up your ass and inspect every inch of this place and we will shut you down for any of the smallest infractions."

The worker's eyes widened and he took a step back away from the woman, who had suddenly become uncomfortably close. "Hey, I'm just doing what the boss tells me to. I'm sorry, I didn't mean to insult you."

"You should've thought about that before," she snapped, turning and walking away.

"You may want to update your resume," said Falau to the worker, with the sternest look he could muster.

"Hey man. I need this job. I have a wife and kids. If I get fired she is going to kill me," pleaded the worker. Falau glanced down at him with rolling eyes.

"I'll see what I can do. She gets hot headed, but to tell you the truth I don't want to spend the next twelve-hours going over all your shipments. Just lay low and I will take care of it and get her to relax," said Falau, extending his hand and patting the man on the shoulder. "You just picked the wrong lady to do that macho bullshit with. She can be crazy when it comes to things like that. She hates men after her divorce."

"I understand. That can be hard on anyone. No problem. Just let me know if you need anything," replied the worker as he walked in the opposite direction back toward the main floor. "I want to work with you guys and make sure everything is fine and keep you and my boss happy."

Falau moved down the aisle quickly to reach Carla and found her paused at an open coffin on the side of the aisle. Her had ran down the side of the coffin like she was inspecting the quality of the work. Her eyes ran over it taking in every detail she could.

"This is how they do it. They pack the drugs in the coffins. These are military coffins, and they have a false bottom. They put the drugs in with the dead serviceman. Nobody in customs would disturb a deceased military member. They take the drugs out at the funeral home when they get the soldier back. You can ship into any of the countries and no one will say a thing. I heard stories about them doing this years ago."

Leaning over the coffin, she ran her hand on the bottom and pushed hard. A small panel opened where the deceased person's right foot would have rested. The sick contraption used for drug smuggling caused the young woman to stare blankly into it. A hand awkwardly rested on her shoulder to comfort her. Falau gave her all the comfort he dared show, unsure of how much was too much.

"That must be the office up there," he said gingerly, while pointing further down the aisle. A set of wooden steps ran up to a door. "He's in there. Perfect place to make our move."

Carla nodded and she walked with quiet confidence to the steps and ascended them quickly. She knocked on the door, standing two vigilant steps to the side for fear of a burst of gunfire coming raking through the door. But the only thing they heard was a voice that said, "Come in."

Pushing open the door, Falau saw two men sitting at a desk reviewing stacks of files, and looking worn down from the task.

"Excuse me. We are the inspectors. Is Mr. Mallarino available?" asked Falau, attempting to sound official.

"Sorry, you just missed him. He went home but he should be back around ten tomorrow morning. You want to leave a message?"

"No need. We just wanted to let him know that the inspection went fine and he could continue as he always has. We will send in a copy of the night's report for his files."

They backed out of the room and down the steps. Moving with purpose they made their way to the front of the warehouse to see The Butcher pulling out of the gate in his car. Knowing there was no way they could take him down now, the couple strolled towards the main gates, watching The Butcher's tail lights disappearing down the main street and into the distance.

NINETEEN

USING his foot to drop the bike into a lower gear, Rivera took the corner without coming to a complete stop, no matter what the sign said. He knew that it was a matter of time before the couple made their move and changed their location, and he wanted to be right on top of them when it happened.

"All right, this shouldn't be too hard," said Rivera to himself inside his helmet.

Bringing the bike, up to the fourth intersection, he took the corner and parked the bike halfway up the block, keeping his eyes peeled for when the couple's car may intersect him once again. Dropping the kickstand to the bike down, the man reached into the inside of his jacket and removed his cellphone from the pocket where it sat. Pulling off his helmet and dropping it on the backseat of the bike, Rivera slid off his gloves and let his thumbs bring the phone to life.

"It seems like the results should be in by now," said Rivera to himself as he worked his way to the employee's website for the National Police department. Opening the site, he moved up, clicking the button to sign in and input all his credentials, letting whoever it be on the other ends of the computer know that he was authorized to enter.

An array of disclaimers popped up on the screen, informing the viewer of how all items on the site were encrypted and that only members of the National Police department would have access to such files. There was also a subtle disclaimer that supervisors and the high members of the National Police system were able to view emails and any other personal information about anybody connected to the police station.

Scrolling to the main page, his thumb looked and finally found the tab for promotions.

Six months before Rivera sat at a desk, working his way through the Commander's exam. Younger than most that sat in the room, but still having the wherewithal to hold his own with any situations presented to him, the young man saw an opportunity with a small class of other officers looking to get the promotion. He worked quickly through the different scenario-ed cases and answered the multiple choice questions without any hesitation at all. The only part that would be a struggle in the future would be the interview process, where issues of his age and anything from his past record could come into play with the authorities who controlled the interview process.

"Oh, God, who knows what this is gonna say?" said Rivera, letting his eyes drift up and look down the road as he heard a car cross through the intersection. The yellow Dodge had no resemblance at all to the car that he was following.

"If it wasn't for that damn interview, I could do the test. It's the other part that kills me."

Drawing in a deep breath, his thumb pushed again,

opening the results for the Commander's exam. Name after name flew by:

Martinez
Garcia
Gomez
Lopez
Gonzalez
Hernandez
Sanchez
Perez

STARING AT THE SCREEN, his name was clearly missing and it was no mistake.

"It figures, I still get some years left," said Rivera to nobody but himself. The blow was difficult but something he knew had been a long shot to begin with. The struggles of a man to move up in a traditional order such as the National Police made it difficult for members in the younger ranks to move up as quickly as they'd like, and they were always told the same thing by the ones that were older, "Your time will come."

Letting his mind drift back to the interview, Rivera reflected on the circumstances that he now felt had held him away from making the next step in his career.

"MR. RIVERA, we're glad that you're able to be here and join us. The only problem we're having is that you're quite a young man compared to the other men. You've attempted to call yourself a contemporary of theirs," said the middle-aged man, with a slightly rounding belly, from behind the desk. He, with one man flanked to the right, and another to the left, were dressed in simple black suits with white shirts and black ties. Nothing was particularly descriptive that showed one man from the other, other than a badge that hung out of the front pocket of their jackets showing who they were with a picture and their vital information to get them in and out of secure areas.

"I understand I'm younger than most men that come in here, but I feel like I've really started to prove myself, and my goal is to spend my life serving the people of Colombia," said Rivera, trying to keep himself from smiling at his good answer.

"Young man, we don't doubt your abilities to work hard and be a credit to the National Police. The problem we have is that it's a certain level of experience that's needed to do the job well. We feel like maybe you just haven't had enough time yet."

"Despite my age, Sir, I've been someone that's been in the thick of most of the major crimes that have been solved here. I feel like I have a second instinct, and I'm sure if you gentlemen talked to me, just for a while, you'll see that I have value," said Rivera, straightening himself in his chair as if preparing himself for the next question to be volleyed to him.

"Well, you're here now, so we might as well have a talk, but I'm sure you know, this is a long shot for anybody," said the man in the center of the other two men behind the table.

"Normally, we wouldn't be doing something like this. We would just dismiss you and ask you to try again later, but a man of your confidence, I feel like we owe it to you to hear what you have to say."

"Thank you for the opportunity, Sir. I hope I can convince you all that I would do a good job," said Rivera, letting himself show the slightest smile. "Please feel free to ask me anything about my life, professional or personal."

"Well, Mr. Rivera, that is one of the things that I would like to discuss with you," said the man behind the desk, as the man to his left pulled the file from his brief case and handed it to him. "Your youth, it seems like there are some things there that are a little bit difficult for us."

"Yes, Sir, I did have some struggles as a young man. My family was very, very poor, and it was up to me to help them make ends meet," said Rivera, again shifting in his chair.

"Well. I have it here that you had been arrested two times, but the charges were dropped. Stealing food both times," said the man staring down at the paper. "My guess is if you got caught twice, there were probably many other times that you did it but didn't get caught."

"Yes, Sir. I'm ashamed to say I did steal things as a young man. I never stole anything for personal gain, it was simply to help feed my family. For me, the idea was horrible even at the time. When I got caught, I wasn't able to help my family at all, but stealing was the only way to get them anything," said Rivera, envisioning in his mind the moment of stealing the loaf of bread when he was only eleven-years-old. The look of the shopkeeper seeing him grab it and the terror that over-fell his body as he ran for the door and then down the street. It had been a moment that he had compromised his ethics in order to do something he knew he was wrong but doing it for the right reason.

"Why didn't you get some other kind of job?" said the interviewer.

"My age prohibited me. I was only eleven-years-old," said Rivera, beginning to feel like the collar on his shirt was getting tighter around his neck.

So you're telling me there was no job available that would supply you with the few pennies that it was needed to buy the small things that you were stealing?" said the man behind the desk starting to shuffle the papers that were within the file. "I see nothing here that even costs over $10."

Letting his eyes make contact with his main interviewer, and then letting them roll to the right and left of him to see the other faces that stared blankly back at him. The three men sat waiting for some kind of an answer that would make sense and justify the act of an eleven-year-old boy who had no idea what to do or when to do it.

"All I can say, Sir, is that at that age, I didn't have the wherewithal to figure out what to do. I had nobody else to help me, no older siblings or parents that were in a position to teach me the right way. It was something I learned on my own through trial and error," said Rivera, knowing that the personal information was revealing more about him than he would have ever allowed under normal circumstances.

"So you're telling you had no concept of what a job was or to work and pay for items. Did you think they were just free for the taking?" asked the interviewer with a snide tone to his voice.

"No, Sir, I did understand about jobs at the time. At the age of eleven though, I wasn't able to do that," said Rivera, having the end of his sentence sharply cut off, despite the feeling that there was so much more to say.

"Well, you must have thought that, Mr Rivera. To have done that shows an absence of knowledge of the world around you," said the interviewer. "You can't expect me believe that you made that choice while still knowing that the right thing to do would be to earn the money. You must have thought you could just take it for free."

"No, Sir," said Rivera abruptly, having a snap in his voice to the man that pressed upon both his intelligence and his integrity.

"Mr Rivera, you stole numerous times. You had time to think about it in between, and you still sit here and insist to us that you had to steal and that you couldn't think of any other way, yet we have established you knew of another way," said the man sitting in the middle as he folded his arms in front of him. "Now, I'm not sure, Mr Rivera, if you're stupid or you're a liar."

The room sat silent for a moment as all parties had taken in what the man had said. If there had been any question before about an attack on his integrity or who he was as a person, it was now complete. There was no area to question what the man meant.

"Sir, with all due respect, you have no idea what I lived through and you have no idea what life was like for me. For you to sit and pass judgment on me is a travesty, Sir!" said Rivera, changing the crossing of his legs from left to right and straightening himself up in the chair while wetting his lips to continue on. "You are trying to tell me what my life was like. You are trying to tell me what I should have done when I was an eleven-year-old boy and scared to death about what might happen. Well, I can tell you, Sir, you have no idea what was happening to me and you have no idea what I am like and how hard I work, and it is inexcusable for you to attack me in such a way."

"Mr Rivera, I will speak to you any way that I choose, I am your superior, not just within the confines of these wall, but in every facet of your life. You are no person to be looked up to. You are no person to be honored," said the man, moving forward on his chair and pointing his index finger firmly at the young man in a jabbing motion. "You and your generation can candy-coat this any way you want, but in the end, we know what was going on. You're a thief and that doesn't go away in just a few years. Once you're rotten to the core, you're always rotten to the core.

"With all due respect again, Sir, you don't know shit!" said Rivera, standing himself up and pulling the bottom of his coat, tightening it to his body. "You have no right to tell me or any other person who they are or what they think. You have no right to pass judgment on anybody... "

"I am your superior! And just as I said before, it is in every way. I will tell you whatever I want, whenever I want, no matter what you think is right. You now need to stand there and acknowledge and say I am your superior," said the man, again waving his finger and viciously pointing at the young man.

"You will get no such thing!" said Rivera. "I have pride in who I am and where I've been, and I have everything I need inside of me to succeed no matter what the job. And this personal attack on me is for no other reason than to try to exclude me from something that I could be a success at. You can't tell me there's not another Commander in this police force that hasn't had arrests as a young man."

Sliding himself down and back into his chair, the

interviewer that had sat in the middle of the two men that flanked him, unfolded in his arms and let them drop down by his side. The angry expression on his face had drifted away as he picked up the chart that sat in front of him.

"I think we have everything we need to know," said the oldest gentleman sitting to the right of the interviewer.

"I think so too," said the interviewer.

"What do you mean? This is it. This is all it is. You come in here and insult me and you wanna leave now? At least stay here and hear what I have to say about my life."

"You don't understand, do you?" asked the man who sat to the left of the interviewer and had been silent until this moment.

"We know that young men have times in their life where they do bad things. If we didn't move men through the ranks that had ever had problems when they were a kid, we'd have nobody in our ranks. But this was a test for you. It was a test to see how you were going to do under pressure. We pressed you on something that should not have made you so intense, and so angry. To be a good Commander, you have to maintain control of yourself. You have to be able to calm things. If you can't take a little questioning about yourself, you'll never make a good Commander."

The three men stood from their chair as Rivera looked across at them, still standing next to his chair. They walked single-file, out of the room, through a back door that they had entered in.

Rivera sat for a moment, realizing that he'd been manipulated and played, all to see how he could handle the real world. His lack of control within an interpersonal situation was going to cost him a promotion, and a fast-track to the hierarchy of the National Police.

Pushing his hair back with his hand, Rivera picked up the briefcase that had lay next to the chair he had been sitting in. Composing himself, he looked back to the seats where the three men had sat. He had blown it, and he knew it. He had been tested and failed, and in short order, proved them right that his maturity had not reached a place that would allow him to be an effective Commander in such an intense atmosphere. As his ego dropped, and depression grew, the young man exhaled loudly, trying to hold back tears that he didn't know were ready to come. The unveiling of who he was, was more than he had ever anticipated when he walked into the interview. His normal history of dazzling those around him, and always being in the top of his class came crashing down from three old men who knew simply how to push the right button to get the response that they wanted. Had he controlled himself, kept on track, and pulled himself together, Rivera knew that the interview would have led to a promotion, but now, instead it was back to the street, and doing the same things, again and again, despite the potential that he had.

TWENTY

DROPPING into the driver's seat, Carla turned the key to bring the car to life.

"Go! Go! Go!" Falau yelled.

The car screeched from the curb and raced up the street, taking a hard-right turn without slowing down. Falau was pleased to have Carla behind the wheel. She was the one who had far more skill when it came to this kind of driving.

Pulling the .45 caliber pistol from his waistband, he checked the magazine to make sure it was full. "Hand me your 9mm," demanded Falau

"It's on my ankle. Just grab it."

Reaching down, Falau lifted the young woman's pant leg and spotted the gun. Taking it from its holster, his hand accidentally rubbed against her skin, reminding him how long it'd been since he felt the softness of a woman.

Opening the magazine, he saw it was filled. He popped it back in and loaded one round in the chamber. Going to the glove compartment he pulled out another magazine, quickly packing one for the 9mm and one for the .45.

"Shit, Carla!" squawked Falau as the car screeched to a harsh stop, but then noticed her eyes were locked on the car in front of them.

"It's him," she said in a calm, soft voice. "He's looking at me in the rearview mirror."

"Change the radio station. Play it cool. Look natural."

Carla reached for the radio as the stop light turned green. The Butcher's car pulled away with his eyes still locked on her in the rearview mirror.

"I don't like this."

"The gas. Pump it a little. Like you're drunk."

The car lurched forward, then settled down as they followed their target from a safe distance. "It's not like he's even looking at the road," she said, a trace of fear in her voice for the first time since she and Falau had met. "His eyes are locked on the mirror, looking right at us. He must know."

"He's on high alert but he has no idea we're after him. Unless the two guys in the office called him." Falau punched the dashboard, in frustration, for not taking more time and care to deal with the office men.

The Butcher's car slowed at another stop light as they pulled up behind. Carla ran her hand through her hair and attempted to look like she was joking with her friend, but all the while she could see the madman looking back examining her. The hum of the motors was the only thing breaking the silence in the crisp air of the night.

The light changed to green and The Butcher pulled away slowly, still looking back at their car.

Carla followed. "He knows. I can see it in his eyes. He's checking out everything I do."

"Calm down. No need to jump the gun with a guy like

this. Let him make the first move," replied Falau. Falau could feel himself starting to work off instinct. His skills with this kind of work were coming back to life, and for the first time in years he felt sure of himself and sure of what he was doing.

"Hold steady on his speed. Let him pull away."

Ten, fifteen, twenty-five, and now thirty-feet ahead, The Butcher edged his car up to the next stop light that turned from green to yellow. He hit the intersection when it turned red and punched the gas, jerking the car forward. The sound of the engine kicking in ripped back to the couple, who saw the taillights suddenly racing into the distance as a red light stared them in the face.

"Fuck it! Go!" screamed Falau.

Pounding the gas Carla pushed the car into high gear, bursting through the traffic coming from the left and the right. Seeing The Butcher two blocks ahead and turning right, she saw the chance to make up time, pushing the car up to 80 miles an hour on the narrow side streets. Stomping on the clutch she dropped the car into third gear and took the corner, trying hard not to fishtail. Tires screeching hard, she had gained on The Butcher.

The sheer power of Carla's Mustang made up the ground and she was suddenly within two car lengths of the madman, who was again looking in his rearview mirror at her.

Falau pulled the .45 from his waistband and opened his window.

"Don't kill him!" Carla demanded looking at Falau and reaching out her arm to grab his shirt.

With her attention on Falau and off from the car in front of her The Butcher saw his opportunity and jammed on his brakes, causing his car to skid.

Carla's eyes darted back to the killer to see the blinding red tail lights shining in her face. Both her feet jammed the brakes hard into the floor, causing her own car to skid, but the momentum was too much and the car crashed into the back of The Butcher's vehicle with a horrendous crunch. Carla spun the wheel looking for any way to control their car, that had totally spun out, pushing them from the road and up onto the sidewalk.

Falau's hand moved his head after banging it hard against the dashboard, cracking the .45 handgun into his skull. Blood dripped from a cut above his hairline and he felt an immediate headache coming on. He was sure it was a concussion, but he had no time to worry about that now.

A sharp pounding sensation hit his mind hard. *It's your fault. You killed me*, echoed through his mind with flashes of his old love covered in blood and looking up at him from the well of the passenger seat.

The Butcher's car lurched to life again after bouncing off a tree and he raced up another block and drove through a gate and up a driveway. The sound of the engine roaring up the long driveway could be heard in the distance as the two pursuers tried to pull themselves together.

"It's now or never. Our cover is blown," said Falau as Carla pulled the car to the side of the road.

Wiping her hand against her mouth she inspected the blood from the now missing tooth. "I can't promise you I won't kill the son of a bitch."

"I know," replied Falau, "and I understand. But if I get him I am going to bring him back."

The beautiful woman nodded her head in agreement, "Fair enough. Let's get him."

TWENTY-ONE

"WHO THE FUCK IS THIS GUY?" said The Butcher sitting at the stoplight and looking into his rearview mirror. "Woman driving, man in the passenger seat. They don't look like they're together, so what that hell are they after following me?"

The Butcher's eyes stayed locked on the rearview mirror taking in the people behind him and waiting to see if they made the next move. By sitting still, he knew that it would cause tension to the situation and bring up the angst in the car behind him.

"If they don't beep, they're following me," said The Butcher to himself in a soft tone, keeping his eyes locked firmly on the driver. Knowing that the normal reaction would be to beep the horn to get him to move through the intersection quicker, The Butcher was sure that if he delayed things, it would call out whether they were simply willing to wait and follow him or make the move that most would in driving around him or leaning on the horn to get him to move.

As the seconds moved by slowly, The Butcher found his eyes locking with the attractive woman in the car behind him. It was unmistakable and there was no denying it. She was attractive and looked as if she was fit, from the little bit of her that he could see. She was unwavering and steady, despite the intense situation. She knew that he was looking at her, and he knew that she knew he was looking at her. The two agreed to simply stare eye to eye waiting to see who would flinch first.

"What are you two talking about? What's going on?" said The Butcher becoming annoyed from the interaction with the people behind him. "Let's see if you guys are up for a chase."

Letting his right foot push down hard on the accelerator, the car jumped off the line and started to race up the street. The car behind him followed in suit but had already given away some distance to The Butcher's vehicle. Weaving in and out of roads and taking multiple intersections that wrapped back in on itself, The Butcher tried to create a tapestry of driving to confuse his followers into where he was intending to go. In a moment like this, where he'd confirmed that they were following him, all he could do was wonder why and find some way to break them from their cause.

Cutting into a four-way intersection, The Butcher leaned on the gas hard as he apexed the turn in the intersection, like a Formula One driver. Cutting off the angle of the turn, he was able to maintain maximum speed and burst up the street that held his home.

"Distance I need more distance." The Butcher muttered to himself watching the car behind him close the distance again.

The people in chase had now pulled to within a car

length opening shooting lanes that left the drug king pin vulnerable.

"How are your reflexes woman!" yelled the mad man slamming his foot to the break causing the car to pull hard to the left fish tailing the back of the car.

The crack of twisting meatal filled the air as the man and woman behind him careened into the back of his car causing them to cut the wheel, looking for control, but only succeeding in spinning the car out and up onto the sidewalk.

Without looking back the Butcher hit the gas getting minimal response to the vehicle that now held a noticeable wobble, in the back left tier, from the impact of the crash.

Arriving at the Butchers home the gates opened, allowing the car to move up the driveway and nestle itself into its waiting spot that it had parked in each day.

"Weapons. I need weapons," said The Butcher as he pushed open the car door and reached to his hip to feel if his .45-caliber revolver sat in its usual spot, waiting to be called into action. It was there as it always had been, ready for the fight. On numerous occasions, the man of such violence had used the gun to dispatch life and cause terror in the people around him. But these folks that were behind him, the ones setting chase to him would need to be made an example of. If they had set the tone to this level and in a public way, he knew that there would be more than one observer who would have noticed his car being chased, and that was something he just could not tolerate. His reputation was too valuable, and it had taken far too many years to build to allow it to go to waste on some punks that were chasing him, more than likely trying to muscle in on his cartel.

"I will gut them alive," said The Butcher, making his way through the garage and into the door of the house. "You come to my home? My home! You come to where I live, not even my place of business, and you're gonna confront me and try to take what's mine?"

Talking to himself had long been a habit that The Butcher had fallen into as a child, more often than not left to play alone and with little to no support from adults. The man had to amuse himself as a child by creating fantasy worlds consisting of happiness that he never found in real life. He had always found it easier to talk to himself and develop his own worlds and his own games, rather than mixing with others who would fight with him over what was right. A short fuse for anger and the quick ability to cause physical harm had the young child quickly labeled as a bully and a bad student. But before he was called The Butcher, he had simply been a young boy with no guidance and no help, he had a course of rage running through him that never seemed to be quenched, and happiness eluded at all turns.

"This is my home!" said The Butcher loudly as he pushed his way through the home, moving to the upstairs where he brandished his weapon and got ready for the fight. "The position had been familiar. He was hidden, tucked away in the home that he lived in, expecting a fight.

The memories flooded back to a time that The Butcher had started his ways. Looking down and noticing the back of his hand, the skin was still rippled from where it had been burned when he was a child. The memories came flooding back without control, letting the man relive a moment that he had wished to forget forever.

"MISS HERNANDEZ, why did you give me this grade on my paper?" asked young Raul to the teacher, as the failing grade stared back up to him from his seat in his fifth grade classroom.

"Raul, you know that the assignment was to complete all the math problems and show all of your work," said Miss Hernandez, moving back to his desk and pointing to the paper that sat in front of him. "You didn't show any of your work, and if I can't see the work, how do I know if you did it right?"

"Well, you know I did it right from the answer," said young Raul, years before he attained the name of The Butcher. "The answers are right there. You don't have any reason to not give me full credit."

"Now Raul, you can see it clearly says in the directions at the top of the paper, you must show all your work," said the teacher, extending her finger and letting it run below the words that were at the top of the page, accentuating her sentence. "I'd be happy to give you half credit on the work if you turn it in again, but only if it has all the work that I can see."

"I did the work in my head, and then I put the answers down on the page. Why do you want me to write it out step-by step if I can do it in my head?" said The Butcher-in-waiting. "The object is to get the right answer, and I'm getting the right answer. Why won't you give me credit for it?"

"Raul, if you would like to talk about this after class, I will be happy to help you then," said the teacher, straightening herself back up and placing her hands on her hips. "Right now it's time for the full class, and we have to move on to our next lesson, but like I just said to you, you can turn the work back in and you will get partial credit."

"I don't want partial credit!" said Raul with his voice raising and his eyes tightening along with his jaw. "I want the credit I deserve for the work I did. I got all the answers right, that's what matters."

"Raul, I told you, we can talk about this after class, this is not the time or place, this is a personal issue for you," replied his teacher, as she reached up to place the pencil into the bun of her hair. "I know you're a very intelligent young man who has a lot going for him. I just want you to see that when we work on these projects, we need to show our work. It will help you later on down the line."

"When am I gonna ever use algebra anyways? I don't need this crap," said Raul, banging his fist down on his desk.

"Young man, I will not tolerate that behavior!" said Miss Hernandez . "You need to take yourself down to the principal's office now. Wait outside his office on the bench and I'll inform him of what went on."

"I'm not going anywhere until I get the credit for the assignment that I did," said Raul, shifting in his seat and staring up at the teacher that towered above him. "Give me my credit now."

"You get to the office now!" said the teacher, pounding the emphasis on the word now. "It's time you learn your place in this classroom and this school. We don't want to have another incident like on the playground."

The playground incident had been all anyone talked about for weeks and almost costing him his placement in the school. Just days before, a young boy had fallen off the top of the slide, and several students had said that Raul had pushed him. The two had a conflict over whose turn it was to use the playground equipment, when Raul had a rage build up inside him causing him to follow the boy up the steps of the ladder to the top of the slide and then push him off the top. The results were a broken clavicle and a shattered kneecap that had yet to see the boy return to school.

"I never pushed him off the slide!" said Raul. "And that has nothing to do with this."

"I said to the principal's office now, Raul!" barked the teacher, causing all eyes to draw to her and several students to shudder in their place. "This is not acceptable. You will behave appropriately in my class and every other class in the school, and if you don't, we will teach you how."

"What do you think? Mr. Mancia is gonna hit me again?" asked Raul. "You think that has any effect on me, that old man whacking me with a paddle? Who cares. When I get big enough, I'm gonna take that paddle right out of his hand and give *him* a few licks with it."

An audible gasp arose from the students in the room. The idea of yielding the discipline paddle that hung on Mr. Mancia's wall and using it against him was unthinkable and a fantasy on a different level than any of the kids had ever had.

"Out now, Raul. The time is over for arguing. Time for you to leave and zip that mouth," said his teacher with her arm extended, pointing at the door.

"Fuck you," said Raul, standing up from his desk and staring with the woman eye to eye. Despite the height difference, the gaze of Raul dug into her and sent a shudder up her spine that she had not felt from any man in her life. Raul's eyes had gone blank, and all that was surviving was the rage he felt inside him.

"I scare you, don't I?" said Raul, pulling his desk to the

side and stepping toward the woman. "You're so much older than me, but you're afraid of me."

"Don't be ridiculous, Raul," said the teacher, stammering at the boy's perception of how she felt. "Now move along to the office. Quickly now. Please."

Sensing the weakness in the woman, Raul took another step closer to her, seeing that she was stepping back with each one of his forward steps. "Do you think I'm gonna hurt you?"

"No, Raul. Of course not. You're not that kind of boy," said his teacher, giving a nervous laugh that nobody in the room accepted as levity. "You just need to follow the rules. A little help, that's all you need, and then we'll get back to things. Now, as I said, come on now, go to the office."

"There's no slide in here. It's not like I can push you from the top of it," said Raul, again stepping in closer as the teacher backed into the wall stopping her progress of stepping backwards. "I could hurt you. I could do a lot of things to hurt you. And you get me so mad that sometimes I feel like I should."

"Look at my hand," said the young boy, showing the ripples of burns on the back of his hand.

"This is what happens when I disobey. My parents have no time for those kinda things. So do you think that by sending me to the principal here and getting a spanking from a paddle can compare to what I have lived?"

Miss Hernandez's eyes looked at the young boy as he pulled himself up tighter to her and stared straight up to her and into her eyes. A fear drove through her as she looked at the back of his hand, where he showed his wounds.

"I can get help for you, but this is a personal matter. We

can talk with the principal about how we can help you if there's anything going on at home," said the teacher.

"I didn't ask for help," said the young man. "If I needed help, I wouldn't get it from you and I wouldn't get it from anybody in the school."

"Well, how about this? We have a conversation about this after class. You can return to your desk for now," said his teacher. "I can see you're very upset by this, and maybe I was a bit too rash by sending you to the principal's office."

"Or we could just finish this right now. You could see if you can make me go to the principal's office," said Raul, staring back up at the woman. "Do you wanna find out? You can run over and make a call to the office. They'll be here in just a few seconds to drag me out. But until then, it'll just be you and me."

"No, no, no," said Miss Hernandez, again stammering, trying to find the right words to control the fear that was building inside of her despite the fact that the young boy was merely half her size.

"I think you owe me an apology," said Raul, raising his finger and pointing it at the teacher. "You owe me an apology, because I did the work and I did it right. If I don't get an apology, then I'm going to have to find some other way to make this right. Maybe you'd like the back of your hand to look like mine."

Again letting her eyes lock on the rippled skin on the back of the young boy's hands, Miss Hernandez looked away as quickly as she had looked at it. It was easier to believe that it had simply been a birth defect rather than abuse. She had turned a blind eye to it all year, knowing that the ramifications of engaging his parents could be far worse than anything else for the young boy.

"I don't think there's any need for that kind of talk, Raul," said his teacher before being cut off.

"I'll decide what I say, not you. Everyone's trying to tell me what to say and how to act, but not anymore."

"I can understand your frustration, so why don't we just move on from this right now, and we'll take care of it all after class," said the teacher.

"I'm not coming back after class. You need to give me my credit. I did the work. Anything less isn't fair," said Raul as his voice tightened with his anger.

"I see. Well, it's something I'll definitely look into," said the teacher.

"You don't need to look into it, you just need to do it," said Raul. "You're going to do it, aren't you?"

All eyes in the room drew to the teacher. The fear was palatable and the shaking in her hands was clear. But the students waited to see what reaction Raul would draw from her and who would win the clash between them.

"Okay. We'll make the adjustment, but from now on, you need to follow the directions," said the teacher looking to the boy with nothing behind his eyes. "I am... I am sorry."

Pulling herself away from the back wall, the teacher moved up the aisle between the rows of seats to the front of the classroom as Raul slowly returned to his seat. Breaking into the next lesson plan, the teacher immersed herself as quickly as she could to pull away from the negative feelings and the difficulty she'd had with the boy.

Sitting in his seat, a smile arose over Raul's face at what intimidation could do. He had learned it well from his father and his mother. The fear of being hit was always much worse than being hit. The fear of discipline and random violence carried more weight than the violence itself. It was a tool that was effective and strong. It could manipulate people and change negative situations into positive situations, and positive situations into negative. The young boy saw the power of intimidation through violence on the playground, and now within the classroom. Nodding his head gently to himself, Raul was perfecting the skill that would be used for the rest of his life, and earn him millions of dollars.

TWENTY-TWO

BURSTING FROM THE CAR, the partners targeted the fence of The Butcher's home. Their feet smacked off the ground as they worked their way to the destination for very different reasons. No matter if it was for revenge or money, they both had just one thing in mind, and that was capturing the madman who had turned killing and intimidation into an art form.

The fence of The Butcher's house was large and made of stone, thus easy to climb with many foot holes and grips for the hands. It was built more for aesthetic value than to keep anyone in or out. Falau crouched down and interlaced his fingers so his partner could slip her foot into them quickly to get a solid boost up the wall. He pushed her up with rapid speed, surprised at how light she was.

Dropping to her stomach on the flat top of the wall she reached down, giving her new friend a hand and helped him up. Falau took her hand quickly, seeing her as an equal in this endeavor. Gender meant nothing to him now. She was his teammate, and despite her femininity, it all left his mind now they were both in attack mode. Carla was the same in every way to him, and he felt he'd never had a finer partner in his life. It was clear to him that anything he could do, she could do just as well. At least that's what he hoped.

Over the wall, the distance to the house looked a difficult course. There were no trees and at least a hundred-yards of slight incline to the back of the house. The ground was grass covered and plush with no places to hide.

"No cover at all," said Carla, slowly shaking her head as she examined the yard. Her jaw tightened and her lips pressed hard together in frustration. "I say we just B-line for the doors by the pool. No use trying to hide. He knows we're here and I'm sure this place is set up with surveillance."

Falau nodded in total agreement and slid down the opposite side of the wall. Right on his heels, Carla did the same. At a full sprint, the team of two ran up the grass hill then pressed their backs against the side of the house, waiting to see if there was any reaction from guards, dogs, or even The Butcher himself, but nothing—or no one—came. Just silence.

"I'll go in by the pool slider doors, but you go to the front of the house. Maybe we can squeeze this rat into a corner by coming at him from two sides."

Falau stared at his partner, unsure if splitting up was the right thing to do. Safety in numbers was always a rule that he lived by. Splitting off alone put them in a situation where they could end up in a one-on-one battle with an extremely dangerous man.

"Are you with me Falau?" snapped Carla.

"Yeah.

"Then stop staring at me and say something. We're kind of in a rush here. Are you good with the plan?"

Nodding his head in agreement Falau said, "Yeah. But if one of us gets in trouble, we yell. Just blow the cover to help each other."

"Done and done. Now go!"

Falau made his way up the embankment next to the house that allowed him a clear view of the driveway. The ground was laid in such a way to make the first floor of the house at ground level in front, and lower to make it ground level at the basement in the back.

Running to the corner he could see the back of the car The Butcher had been driving. The sharp pain of a flashback kicked inside his head.

"Not now!" he grunted to himself, keeping his feet moving and his mind on what needed to be done.

The car wasn't parked in any intentional way. It was half turned sideways and the garage door was open. The Butcher must've raced up the driveway, stopped the car as fast as he could and ran into the garage. But was he still in there?

Sliding out the .45 caliber handgun from the soft holster tucked into the back of his waistband, Falau held the gun deliberately in front of him and crept forward. He had a clear view of the far side of the garage, but Falau was blind to what lay closest to him, out of sight due to the corner. The garage was three-cars wide and held a Mercedes, a Porsche, and now the crushed BMW.

Too many places to hide, he thought moving forward into the corner. I could walk right into him.

Falau rolled around the corner and dropped to one knee with the weapon straight out in front of him, revealing the closest section of the garage. Nothing.

He moved in and searched, in and out of the cars, but saw nothing that provided a clue to where The Butcher was.

Only one thing was sure, and that was that The Butcher was not hiding in the garage.

On the back wall three steps led up to a door that had been left ajar. Sliding to get a glimpse of what lay inside, but still keeping a safe distance, all that could be seen was a tile floor that ran up to the threshold. It was a hallway. *People tend not to tile the inside of closets,* thought Falau.

Climbing the steps to the door he looked deeper inside and found only darkness. The Butcher was drawing him further into the house. He knew the layout of the house. He knew where the furniture was. He knew the places to hide. In the dark, they would be vigilantes who would have to move at a snail's pace to not bump into anything and give the killer a reference point to shoot at.

Slipping through the door a twenty-foot hallway stretched in front of him, and opened into a large kitchen. Try as he might to be silent, Falau still created ample sound in the silence of the house as his shoes echoed off the tile floor. There was a door on the opposite wall of the counters. It was glass. Inside the door the steps were covered in carpet, and led down to the basement.

Moving to the far end of the kitchen he found a set of French doors already open, which led to a sunken living room and a plush carpet to muffle the sound of his footsteps.

The living room was wide open. A sectional sofa lined the back and side wall. There was nowhere to hide in this room. It was designed for entertainment, but could also give a clear shot to anyone moving across it. Keeping to the wall was the safest bet. Walls will cover your back as long as you keep your eyes sharp. Moving in front of the TV, that was laid into the wall with a custom-built entertainment center, Falau could see that the stairs came down as he got to the other side of the room. The steps were covered in carpet, but the chance of them creaking was difficult to assess. Getting caught in the middle of a set of steps was the worst of all situations; nowhere to run or hide. Trapped, with just up or down to choose from while bullets flew your way from those same two directions? No good! There was really no choice. Upstairs had to be searched, and now was the time.

Up two, three, five, eight steps, with all the sound of a church mouse. Yet Falau still feared the creak or moan from the steps would give away his position.

Creak!

From down the steps and around the corner the sound of an un-oiled hinge landed firmly in the ear of Falau. "The basement door," he whispered to himself.

But was it Carla coming up, or The Butcher going down? The risk was too big to wait and find out. Falau moved back down the steps with purpose, though as stealthy as he could in the situation. Running into a trap filled with gunfire was not what he wanted to do. His feet slid across the living room rug and he stopped at the corner.

If tactics had taught him anything, it would be that The Butcher would be waiting with his gun sited on him as he turned the corner. Taking a deep breath and pressing his back against the wall, he revealed himself as he burst around the corner and dropped to one knee.

"Freeze!" screamed Carla from one floor below.

As the words registered with Falau he heard two shots ring out from the basement. Without hesitation, he ran to the basement door in the kitchen and swung it open. Flying down the steps he could hear the backslider of the basement slam shut and the sound of heavy feet crossing the cement that surrounded the pool and fading into the distance.

The basement was another location for entertainment, with a bar and a pool table, but next to the pool table laid a body, motionless and unmistakably the shape of a woman.

With his heart rate quickening with fear and his vision blurring with tears, Falau moved as fast as he could to Carla. No longer worried about getting shot at or completing the mission, he had only one thing on his mind, and that was saving his new partner.

Sliding to his knees and stopping right next to her he could see her gasping for air as blood streamed from her mouth.

He soon spotted a red spot on her shirt, increasing in size as the seconds wore on. It was on the left side of her chest close to her heart.

"You're okay!" said Falau out of instinct, and he placed his hand over her wound trying desperately to stop the bleeding.

"I will get you out of here! You're fine!"

"No... I am... not," said Carla with a faint smile and looking into the eyes of Falau. She placed her hand onto his, the one trying to stop the bleeding. Grabbing it tight she moved it away from the wound and squeezed it. "Make this worth it."

"What?" Falau asked, leaning closer.

"Make this worth it. For my brothers."

Blankness settled on his face as he looked down at his dying friend. She knew her fate and she wasn't fighting. She coughed hard as the blood filled her lungs and shot from her mouth. Falau held her body tight in his arms as she trembled until she trembled no more.

TWENTY-THREE

AS CARLA'S head was laid to rest on the carpet of the basement floor, the sound of the creaking door and footsteps coming down the steps signaled to Falau that The Butcher was coming.

Falau picked up Carla's Ruger SR9C 9mm handgun and tucked it into his waistband for safe keeping. If he could not save her at least he could take some small part of her to remember her by.

Ducking behind the pool table, he held his pistol tight.

Bang!

A shot cut through the air, ricocheting off the slate top of the pool table and embedding in the wall.

"Who are you? What do you want with me?" questioned The Butcher with more hate in his voice than confusion. "You know how many cops I've killed? You think I'm afraid to kill a cop? If you run now you may have a chance to get away. I am not as fast as I once was."

"I was sent to offer you a deal," said Falau attempting to

pull the man's emotions and get his mind working on something other than where he was.

"The kind of deal where you attack me? I'm not a fool. You're here to kill me," said The Butcher. "It would be easier just to kill you and feed your remains to the lions at the zoo."

The sound of footsteps retreating back up the stairs and was clear as day. The Butcher wanted a game of cat and mouse. He could work the room, drawing his prey into the open. If he had chosen his footsteps would have been soft and undetected. But the sound was intentional just begging Falau to run after him.

If he had a cell phone with him, Falau was sure that guards would already be on their way. When they arrived they would come heavily armed and with no fear of being arrested. The Butcher had taken care of that with bribes years before. The time to make a move was now, or the moment would slip away forever.

Arriving at the steps he used his gun to sweep across, making sure he was clear. The door had been left open at the top of the steps. Falau stopped shy of running through it and held back. He knew better, and took his time again. He started at one side of the room and worked his way across, looking through the site of his pistol. *Cut the room like a pie* his old Sargent would say. *Take it one slice at a time making sure everything is secure.* Once there was no more room to secure you were free to move forward. Only a fool would rush though a doorway in a fire fight or someone who had not been trained in the art of close quarters warfare.

Bang!

A shot splintered the door frame on the far side where Falau stood. Checking the angle of the impact into the doorframe, he worked out the shot had come from the living room. It was a slip by The Butcher. He had given away his location. Falau finally turned the gun around the corner, firing two shots to provide himself with cover. After firing the shots, he slid across the floor behind the kitchen island. His location was blown by the simple sound of his shoes hitting the tile floor, but the island provided more secure cover. If The Butcher were bold he could make a rush and try to catch him off guard, but that was a long shot. The island could be moved around and provide the cover for Falau. The Butcher held more skill than that.

"You shouldn't have killed her. That was a big mistake! It changes everything," said Falau, trying to draw a response from the killer so he'd give up his position. The home was well furnished and curtains hung from the windows. The acoustics would kill any echo and give away the location of his pray.

"Why? Did you love her?" said The Butcher letting his voice go gentle for a moment.

Pausing and quickly putting together his thoughts, he knew the answer was not that clear-cut. It was not love or hate, or anything so juvenile. It was deeper, despite the limited time he knew her. There had been no time to even think about love, or even if Carla had any interest in him. She had been his partner and the first woman he had cared for in years.

"No. Much worse than love. I respected her," Falau called back, feeling a lump in his throat. It had been so long since he had respected anyone, including himself. His life had been filled with a series of rejects and losers for the last five years. Carla had changed that. She had purpose, honor, and passion for what was right, even if she had to do the wrong thing to make it right. "You're going to pay for what you have done."

"You sound like a man of passion," said the Butcher calmly. "I can see why you cared for her, she was beautiful. I did her a favor by shooting her. If I had caught her alive she would have been a play thing for my boys on the street."

Reaching down Falau removed his shoes, placing them on the floor behind the island. Inching forward to the front of the island, his eyes started to adjust to the darkness, his footsteps now silent with nothing but a sock touching the floor.

The Butcher was not on the right side of the living room. "Too bad you're not smart enough to run. But it's survival of the fittest. The stupid must die for us all to get stronger," called the voice now coming from the far side of the living room.

Quickly moving to the edge of the double doorway, Falau again started to cut the room with his gun. Slow and methodical, checking every inch. No mistake could be afforded now he was this close. Despite The Butcher's words he knew that this night would end up with one of them dead. He would fail in his mission, but maybe he could avenge Carla's death.

He stepped down to the living room, training his gun at the banister that ran down the wall next to him, ending at the far end of the room. If the chance of a shot came, he would take it. Shoot him dead. One shot, two shots, three shots... it didn't matter. Just end the sorry son of a bitch's life and be done with it.

"Never thought a guy called The Butcher would run and hide. Such a coward," called out Falau, waiting for a response. But The Butcher was not saying a word, keeping his location hidden.

Getting down low, Falau crept close to the wall below where the banister came down. The killer's voice was not coming from above... his last words were from the adjoining room, waiting for Falau to show himself and walk straight into the line of fire, Falau was sure that The Butcher was waiting for him.

Suddenly, from over the banister flew a man with a great scar running down his cheek, and The Butcher crashed down, knocking Falau to the ground and causing Falau's gun to fly from his hands.

The Butcher quickly wrapped a cord around Falau's neck, and tightened it as hard as he could. Falau forced his fingers into the loop, slipping them under the cord and trying to keep the blood flowing to his head.

"You're going to learn why they call me El Carnicero! No easy death, not like with the girl. I am going to put you on display for everyone to see."

His face pressed hard into the side of Falau's face, as spit shot from his mouth and sweat dripped from his head.

The feeling of panic started to overwhelm Falau from a lack of oxygen. He'd felt this way once before when he was a young boy. He went swimming in the ocean and was pulled under by the waves, looking for air when there wasn't any there.

He tried to throw his elbows back at his attacker and kick him, but it had little effect. The man was too strong and the cord was doing its job.

The cord started to cut into his neck. His fingers were doing nothing to prevent cutting off the circulation. Falau's eyes started to roll in his head and his world began to turn gray.

"I'm not going to kill you now. I'm going to keep you alive and just kill you a little bit each day in my basement. Let you look at that whore of a friend. This is what happens to people who want to confront The Butcher. You will be lucky to have died by my hands."

The sound of a gun cocking stopped the words spilling from The Butcher's mouth. His grip loosened. Falau pulled the cord away from his neck and dropped to the ground on his hands and knees, gasping for air. Color flooded back into his vision and his head felt clearer again.

"Get up and stand against the wall with that piece of trash," commanded the voice.

"Who the hell are you?" asked The Butcher, pointing his finger at the man.

"My name is Carlos Rivera, with the National Police Special Operations Commandos. Now shut the hell up."

Falau pulled himself up and looked at the man from the National Police. He was young and brash. Falau immediately liked him.

"You're a cop?" he asked.

"National Police."

"Sorry. I'm kind of in the same line of work that you are, but more of a bounty hunter. I have some people that want to see this guy on trial for all the drug running."

"That's fine, but you two are going to jail until I find out who killed the girl. Somebody's going to pay for that."

"Let me take the sick freak out of here, and I can make sure he pays."

"Shut up!" demanded Rivera. "You really think I will let the two of you walk out of here?"

"I have one-million in cash and will give it to you now if you let me leave. Do with him what you will," interjected The Butcher.

Shaking his head Falau again turned his attention back to the National Policeman.

"Can I shut this guy up for us?"

"Sure."

Removing the small injection kit from his shirt collar—just where Tyler said it would be—he jabbed it into the neck of The Butcher, causing the killer to lash out at him. Rubbing his neck, the killer pulled the needle from his neck and he fell to the floor.

"That's better," said Falau.

"Why do they want him? The people you work for?"

"He's killed a lot of people with the drugs he's smuggled. He cuts it with Carfentanil. They want to give him another trial which is not so public."

"You know I can't let him just walk away."

"I understand," replied Falau, rubbing his chin with his thumb and finger. "But what if I could give you something more valuable than this jerk. What if I can hand you the biggest drug bust in the history of Colombia?"

The National Policeman stood still and trained his gun on Falau. He was weighing his options and deciding if he could trust him.

"It's a simple choice. You could shoot me or you could be a huge hero. It's up to you."

Carlos Rivera lowered his gun and smiled. "Tell me what you know."

TWENTY-FOUR

PULLING down to the loading bay, the hearse backed up, bumping its backdoor against the rear entrance to McGinty's Funeral Parlor. The engine shut down and the driver slid the door open.

Stepping from the hearse Falau looked up to the sky, seeing few stars. "Miami, you kill the stars with the streetlights."

Walking up to the door, he knocked in the specific pattern he had been instructed to by Tyler. Knocking out the signal let the men inside know it was him. Slowly the metal door slid open, revealing two large men who stepped forward and opened the back of the hearse without saying a word.

"Hey old friend," chirped Tyler inside the doorway. "Congratulations on your first successful mission."

"Thanks," Falau responded in a somber tone. "There was a heavy price to pay."

"I heard. She was one of the best. My guess is he hit her with a lucky shot."

"Not lucky for her."

"No."

Tyler held his hand out, making sure Falau knew he was happy with the work he had done.

"You did an amazing job. Carla knew the risks but wanted to be part of this one. She would be proud of you. You made him pay for her death and the deaths of a lot of other people."

Falau looked to the floor and grunted in passive agreement. He wasn't sure how he felt about the whole thing. People were now dead and nothing could bring them back.

"Come inside," said Tyler with a wave of his hand.

"I'm just going to head back home."

"No! Come on man, just come in for a few minutes and have some coffee."

Tyler wrapped his arm around his friend and led them into a hallway now half covered by the coffin that had been in the back of the hearse.

"Is he in there?" asked Tyler.

"Yeah. He started to stink."

"I know. It's disgusting. But that's what happens."

Tyler placed his hands on the coffin, pushing it off its perch on the rollers. The wooden box hit the floor, smashing on the concrete, before the body of The Butcher tumbled onto the floor.

The killer's eyes locked on the men around him, as he struggled to get free of the bonds that tied his hands and feet. His mouth was covered in duct tape.

"Men, take out the trash to the main room. It's time for trial."

"Trial? Now?"

"Yeah, the judges are here. This will all be over in just a few minutes. By the way, everyone is very impressed you used one of his smuggling coffins to ship him back."

"I thought it was a nice touch," said Falau with a smile as they walked to the open door at the end of the hallway.

TWENTY-FIVE

THE ROOM WOULD NORMALLY HOLD wakes, but had been cleared of the normal chairs and tables. Under where the casket normally sat there was a single chair The Butcher was positioned in. A single muted light bulb shone down upon him. A crucifix hung on the wall behind him, looking down on him during this time of his judgment. To his right along the wall sat nine empty high-backed chairs, but none of the people in the room made a move to occupy them. Clearly they were for the judges.

On the opposite side of the room were a few people in attendance. Falau, Tyler, four other men, and two women, who made no attempt to interact with anyone at any time. The operation was all business... there was no time for anything but the task at hand.

One of the larger men walked over and ripped the tape from The Butcher's mouth, taking part of his facial hair with it.

"Fuck you!" screeched The Butcher, spitting on the man who ripped the tape from his mouth. "Let me go, I swear I

179

will kill you all. What the hell is this, playtime for you people? Get me the fuck out of here!"

"Silence. You will have your chance to speak," responded the man now covered in spit.

"Let me go!"

In one smooth motion, the man spun back to The Butcher and jammed a revolver into his mouth. "I asked you to be silent, and told you that you would have a chance to speak. Do you understand me this time?"

The Butcher nodded as his eyes focused on the man's finger lightly dusting over the trigger.

"Good. Thank you."

Removing the gun from his mouth, the man walked away, as The Butcher took a deep breath and examined the room. Making eye contact with Falau at the far end, he stared hard.

Falau lifted his glass, as if he was toasting the man. "I don't think he likes me."

"Think you're right. But he seems like he could be a hard guy to get along with," Tyler responded with a smirk.

On the far side of the room a door slid open, and silence fell across the room. All eyes moved to the door, waiting with anticipation. Falau did as all the others did, but had no idea why. The feeling that something would be missed if he looked away was overwhelming.

One by one, nine people entered the room. They ranged in height and weight, but they all had one thing in common; you could not see any part of their bodies. All the judge's robes covered them from their neck to their feet, including their arms. It was impossible to see their hands. A hood even covered their hair, while black and white masks covered their faces. Falau thought they looked like the comedy and tragedy masks you'd see at the theater. The difference was, these masks all had different expressions on them, everything from horror to happiness. It was impossible to detect any real emotion from any of the judges wearing the uniform they had devised.

The judges found their seats and sat down, and still they didn't speak. They looked straight ahead and interacted with nobody in the room. Falau knew without being told that the judges were off limits. There was to be no friendly chitchat. No asking how the family was, or if they're enjoying their stay. Their anonymity was paramount and nobody was going to get in the way of that.

"Step back against the wall," requested Tyler. "We can't interfere in any way or he goes free. The rules are very strict to make sure everything works out for the best."

Leaning back against the wall, Falau thought if they let the sick piece of garbage go after all he went through to get him, and especially after Carla died, he would lose his mind.

A man in his late fifties stepped to the center of the room. He wore a well-fitting suit that looked to be in the $300 range. Nice, but off the rack and not custom-made. Life had taken its toll on the man. He bore deep wrinkles and thinned hair that was approaching fully gray. He stood with a slight hunch and needed reading glasses, the kind that many old folks wore in the movies that sat at the end of their noses. Despite running over the various situations in his head, Falau could come up with no reason that would explain how this man ended up working with this kind of group. How was he involved with the judges and bringing people to justice?

The man cleared his throat and raised his hand, showing that he wanted silence in an already silent room.

"Good evening. You have decided to bear witness to the

trial of Raul Mallarino, otherwise known as The Butcher." The man moved his hand, indicating the man tied up against the wall.

"What kind of shit is this? I had a trial and was found innocent," squawked the stone-cold killer.

"Sir, I informed you that you will have a chance to speak. I do not want to have to muzzle you for the rest of these proceedings."

The Butcher snorted with contempt, but resisted speaking out again. Falau was impressed this man could shut The Butcher up with words, and not the insertion of a pistol into his mouth as the other man had used.

"Sir, you are hereby charged with drug trafficking, murder, murder by drug trafficking, criminal conspiracy, corruption of government officials, and you are fully responsible for the deaths of 384 Floridians in the last two years, due to drugs you bring into the area cut with Carfentanil, and countless deaths in Columbia. How do you plead?"

The Butcher squinted his eyes and tilted his head to the side. "How do I plead? You want to know how I plead? I was tried by my home country of Colombia and found innocent. This isn't even a courtroom! You have me in a funeral home for the trial, so you can just kill me and dump me in a grave! Well, screw you all!"

"Sir, do you plead innocent or guilty? If you do not provide a plea, we'll take your silence as a plea of guilt."

The man in the suit stared at The Butcher. "Your answer, Sir? Now."

"You people are insane! I'm innocent! Innocent of everything they say I have done!" snapped The Butcher, struggling to break the binds that held his hands.

"The plea is innocence. The questions will now start." The man in the suit walked over to the judges and made his way to the one that sat last in line. A gloved hand slid out from under the robe holding a stack of index cards, and handed them to the man, pointing to the top one. Without any conversation, the man in the suit moved back to the center of the room and faced The Butcher.

Falau watched the interaction intently and realize the judges spoke to nobody. Nothing about their identity was going to be known to anybody, even the sound of their words. He wondered if Tyler was the only one who had any real contact with the judges.

"Sir. Have you ever trafficked drugs to the United States?"

"Ever?"

"Sir, please answer the questions as they are asked. Have you ever trafficked drugs to the United States?"

"Yes. I was a young man. Just one time. My family needed the money for—"

"A simple yes or no will do," interrupted the man in the suit.

"Did you traffic drugs into Miami?"

"Yes, the one time—"

"That's good," interrupted the man in the suit again.

"Did you ever cut your drugs with Carfentanil?"

The Butcher looked over to the judges and then scanned the room. His face hardened as he nodded. "You all think you're so much better than me but I do what I have to, to survive. I pulled myself up from nothing and look what I have achieved. Now you think you can pass judgment on me?"

"That's exactly what these judges are here to do,"

snapped the man flipping to the next card. "Did you sell your drugs to Juan Martinez in Miami?"

"Yes! So what? What does it matter if I did? It was his choice who he sold the drugs too. He was the one killing people by pushing it on the streets."

"Martinez is dead. He tested his shipment. Not even a large amount, but it killed him."

Watching The Butcher's face go blank, Falau could see for the first time he had been shaken.

The Judge who had given the index cards raised his hand into a 'stop' position. The man in the suit walked back to the judge and handed the index cards to him. He also handed a small piece of paper to each judge and returned to the center of the room.

"The judges will now deliberate, and we will have a verdict momentarily."

"Wait a minute! He said I would have a chance to speak. I want to say some things!"

"You did have a chance to speak. You had your say when you answered the questions. That's all they needed to hear from you."

A tapping sound emanated from the head judge as his foot repeatedly hit the floor, stopping the conversation. The man walked back over and collected the paper from the judges. Placing himself back at the center of the room, he held the card in front of him and looked down his nose through his glasses to read the fate of The Butcher.

"The judges have come to a unanimous verdict."

On those words, the judges stood up in unison and marched single file out the same door they entered through. Falau was sure they would be gone from the premises well before any action was taken.

"On all accounts, you have been found guilty as charged. Sentence will only be carried out on the charge of the deaths of 384 people as a result of drug trafficking, and of cutting the drugs with a known lethal substance."

"You can't do this! You have no right to find me guilty of anything! I want a lawyer!"

"You are hereby sentenced to death within the next hour, and may God have mercy on your soul."

"What? No! You can't—" The Butcher was silenced by a strip of duct tape over his mouth. Struggling back and forth, he fell to the floor in a panic and several men converged on him and removed him from the room.

"Ladies and gentlemen," said the man in the suit. "Justice has been served. Let's go now and forget anything ever happened here. Take care."

The man with the simple suit and years of work etched into his face tucked his glasses into the front pocket of his jacket and walked out the door.

TWENTY-SIX

THE DOOR of the coffee shop, two buildings down from Falau's apartment, swung open with a hard push from Falau.

Entering the shop, he ran his eyes over the room and saw Tyler sitting at the furthest booth. Tyler always placed himself in a position of power by facing the door and having his back to the wall. Nobody could sneak up on him from that position. Was it intentional, or was it just habit at this point for his friend to be on high alert?

Scanning his eyes over everyone in the room, Falau felt his senses were once again alive. He was running on instinct, and the sharpness of his mind was fantastic. The room was safe and he knew it. He knew the people who were the greatest risk, and he knew those who were not. He knew who had a gun and who didn't. He was back on track in every sense of the word, despite the difficulties he'd witnessed.

"How are things going?" said Falau, sliding into a seat opposite his old friend.

"Things are always great when the world becomes a safer

place overnight," smirked Tyler as he raised a cup of coffee, using it to point at the TV, set high above the counter.

The national news was showing a smiling man standing in front of a mountain of cocaine. He held up two automatic weapons and was awash in the flashes of camera bulbs exploding in his face. Across the bottom of the screen a banner with yellow letters surrounded by red, read: *'Lt. Carlos Rivera of the National Police of Colombia makes the biggest drug arrest in the history of South America.'* A handsome man came back to the TV broadcasting live from Colombia. "More than two-thousand kilos of cocaine and over one-hundred kilos of heroin were confiscated in the early morning hours at the Jetway International import and export facility in Bogotá, Colombia. The result of this massive confiscation could limit the sales of drugs all over the United States and Europe."

"That's one happy cop," said Tyler with a smile. He took a sip of his coffee and placed it on the table.

"National Police. I hear they are touchy about that kind of thing..." said Falau.

"That should put him on the fast track to the top command. He could be a good man to know if you're ever in that part of the world. Who knows what he could help a guy with in the future?"

Tyler was right. Rivera was now a major contact, and someone who was willing to work with him if the price was right and if Falau could provide him with another big bust. If the judges were big on getting smugglers in Colombia, this was going to be an outstanding contact.

"Yeah he would be."

Tyler shifted in his seat and reached for his briefcase. Flipping the locks to open it, he removed a plain brown oversized envelope, the kind that most offices use for interoffice mail. He placed the envelope on the table and slid it across to Falau.

The envelope was thick, and sealed closed with red twine that linked around two red circles attached with string.

"This is for you."

Picking up the envelope, Falau opened the top and could see inside several small packs of money. All US currency, in denominations of $10, $20, and $100 bills that all looked used and dirty. There was no way they were counterfeit or had markings of any kind of sequential order. Nothing about the money would link him to the judges in any way. They were perfectly random.

"Thanks," said Falau, wrapping the red string around the circles again. "Feels good to be on the side of the good guys. I was starting to wonder if I was still one of the good guys now."

"Falau, there was never any doubt in my mind that you were still one of the good guys."

A large heavy-set waitress, wearing a nametag reading Helen, stood at the end of the table. "You want something to eat?" she grunted at Falau.

"Tell me something..." Tyler glanced up to read the nametag. "...Helen. Looking at this guy right now, would you say he is one of the good guys?"

"My name ain't Helen. It's Ruth. I forgot my nametag today. He's a good guy if he leaves a good tip. Want coffee or food?"

"Coffee is fine," said Falau with another smile.

"Great, I'm sure there will be a good tip on a ninety-nine-cents cup of coffee," moaned Ruth as she walked away from the table.

"See, even Ruth knows you're one of the good guys, and you always have been. You've just had some tough times."

"Wish I could believe that. Maybe in time I can see things right."

"You can do it with us. If this is the work for you, I've been told it's okay to give you more assignments. You wouldn't exactly be part of the inner circle, but you would play a vital role in the success of the operation."

Falau looked down at the table and placed his hands behind his neck. He rubbed hard, as if he was trying to ease away a muscle knot.

"I don't know. I almost got myself killed down there. If not for some luck I would've failed."

"But you didn't. You succeeded. For whatever reason, you came out on top. That's all that matters. You're getting your chops back. You're like a great jazz musician. You just can't pick up from where you left off after not playing for years and try to sit down with Miles Davis and knock out a few tunes. It takes time. I know you don't like to talk about your past but you need to accept it. It's who you are."

"I don't know what to tell you."

"Tell me you'll think about it. No need to decide here and now. Just call me if you could use some work, even if it's only part-time." Tyler reach into the pocket of his suit jacket and pulled out a card very similar to the one he gave Falau before. The only writing on it was the phone number.

"Take care of yourself, my friend. Was great seeing you again," said Tyler as he stood up and placed his hand on Falau's shoulder, squeezing it while looking down into his eyes. "Just don't wait too long if you want to be on the job. My bosses tend to like consistency, and to know what's going on all the time. I will hold the spot as long as I can. The Fixer can't take forever."

"Is that what the judges call me? The Fixer," Falau said with a wide smile.

"No. I am The Fixer. I fix problems and I can't take forever to get back to them," explained Tyler with a slight laugh. "Take care."

Tyler patted Falau's shoulder one last time and walked towards the door. Falau looked at the card in his hand and spun it between his fingers. Even with all the risk and Carla's death, Falau was feeling better now than he had in years. The flashbacks had been gone for almost a week and his drinking had slowed. He felt like he had something to live for, and that was a feeling that had left him a long time ago.

"Where did your buddy go?" Ruth said, placing the coffee in front of Falau with a small splash. "Hun. He didn't even leave you with a few bucks to cover the cost of his coffee. Some friend he is."

Ruth rumbled away, her words echoing in Falau's ears, "Some friend he is." And she was right. He is some friend. The kind of friend that looks after you when you're at the worst point in your life. One who comes in and bails your ass out when you're getting ready to end it all.

That kind of friend is a best friend.

Pulling the cell phone from his pocket Falau quickly dialed the number on the card, stopping Tyler right outside the coffee shop.

"Ya... Tyler."

"Falau. Stay there."

Falau shoved some money on the table and jumped up, moving to the door as fast as he could. Pushing the door open, he tried not to run to Tyler and cause too many eyes to look at his old friend. Falau detected at least two cars in the area he was sure Tyler would soon be followed by. Quickening his pace, he reached Tyler and caught his breath.

"One more assignment, just to see how things go."

Extending his arm, Tyler smiled as Falau shook hands with him. "Falau, I feel really good about this."

Suddenly they heard screaming from inside the coffee shop. Falau and Tyler turned to look, and saw Ruth crying and holding the hundred-dollar bill Falau had left for her.

Falau shrugged his shoulders. "She earned it with her sunny disposition."

ABOUT THE AUTHOR

Jack Walker, author of action-packed thrillers, is a man of enigmatic prowess whose roots trace back to the heartland of America. Born and raised in the sprawling hills of Virginia, Walker developed an unyielding love for storytelling amidst the region's rich history and landscapes.

Having a penchant for intricate plots and adrenaline-pumping narratives akin to the stylings of his author hero's, Walker has entered the literary arena after a distinguished military career that exposed him to the clandestine complexities of global conflicts and the subtle undercurrents of espionage.

A graduate of the United States Naval Academy, Walker seamlessly transitioned to the high-stakes world of intelligence and black ops. His experiences, akin to the protagonists he pens, have carried him across continents, brushing shoulders with characters as diverse as the storylines he crafts.

Drawing inspiration from the explosive action of Clancy's techno-thrillers, the intricate plots of Ludlum, the relentless pacing of Flynn, and the tactical precision of LT Ryan, Jack Walker's narratives transport readers into the heart of modern warfare and international espionage.

A man in his late 40s, Walker currently resides in a quiet farmhouse nestled in the Virginia countryside, surrounded by the very landscapes that fuel his imagination. It's here where he meticulously constructs his next gripping saga, drawing from his rich tapestry of real-life experiences and in-depth knowledge to shape the destiny of his bold and resilient characters.

facebook.com/mikegomesauthor

ALSO BY JACK WALKER

<u>The Fixer Series</u>

The Fixer

While Collar

9MM

Piranha

Holiday

Down Under

Gods Executioner

Combat Zone

Printed in Great Britain
by Amazon